MINE FOR THE Night

NEW YORK NIGHTS
BOOK ONE

KIA CARRINGTON-RUSSELL

Mine for the Night

ISBN (ebook): 978-0-6451320-5-2

ISBN (Paperback): 978-0-6451320-6-9

This is a work of fiction. Similarities to real people, places, or events are entirely coincidental.

CRYSTAL
◆ PUBLISHING ◆

A special thank you to all the phenomenal women in my life. So many of you have supported me in reinventing myself as an author and making some drastic changes that I might've been too scared to make without your encouragement. Thank you for your love and support and know that I'm always cheering for you. Thank you x

Chapter 1

Damon

"You can only stay in hiatus for so long, Damon," Alex remarked. Surely, he had better things to do at 10:00 p.m. on a Friday night in Manhattan than stay back in the office with me. I leant over my polished wooden desk and served him another whiskey, which he held no complaints for.

I loosened my tie, the conversation already feeling like it was strangling me. It was a similar conversation I'd had with my sister as she came and checked up on me after hearing the news. The only difference is she had less tact. Alex worked for me, so he always watched his tone.

I ignored him, as I had my sister. This was one conversation I wanted no part in yet. Behind me,

Manhattan soared with flashing lights and commotion, lively as always. *The city that never slept.* So much entertainment, and yet I found comfort hiding in the depths of my office, brooding over the article my sister, Michelle, brought to my attention. *Their names had been the last I wanted to read about.*

I threw back the rest of my whiskey, enjoying its burn, ignorant to a barrage of my brooding thoughts. "Don't you have somewhere else to be, Alex?" Surely, he'd rather be anywhere else other than here while I sulked.

He seemed almost offended. "I wanted to make sure you're okay."

"You only get paid until five," I remarked dryly. He flinched. It was cold, even for me, but I wanted to be alone. This was my issue, not his.

"You're right," he said, picking up his long cream coat. "I'll see you on Monday. And try to do something with yourself this weekend, Damon. You can only let yourself be consumed by work for so long."

"Did my sister tell you to say that?" I edged.

"No just a concerned friend," he said, deflecting the jab.

I circled my thumb over the edge of the crystal glass, unwilling to meet his gaze. I was getting tired of these pep talks as of late.

Silence consumed me, as best as it could with the city a constant turbulent noise at my back. A low buzz grated inside my desk. Frowning, I pulled out the drawer on my right. Who would be contacting this cell? I hadn't handed out a business card for my services in months. I unclipped it from the charger, the only reason why it was still active. How long had it sat forgotten in my desk?

A simple text from an unrecognized number. *Is this Damon?*

I sat the phone down and poured myself another drink, curious by who might've been on the other end. It wasn't practical for me to respond since I'd decided to stop my nightly services a long time ago. And yet, an instinctual pull had me leaning over my desk to dial the same number. Maybe it was my current mood or simple intrigue that got the better of me.

"Hello?" a voice shakily answered on the other end. I leant back in my chair, a smile appearing. Was she... nervous?

"Do you need to be escorted somewhere?" I asked huskily, enjoying her mouselike tone.

"Um." I could imagine her licking her lips. Her throat sounded dry. Definitely nervous. She did know what she was calling for didn't she? "I do It's a... a formal event."

"I only do masquerade," I countered.

"It is masquerade," she blurted out, stunning me for a moment. It wasn't the mousey woman who answered but one of sheer determination. How interesting. "Tomorrow night?"

I mulled over the idea, my finger playing with the edge of my glass again. I hadn't taken a client on in months. It was risky, and yet for some reason, I felt riveted by the thought. For the first time in a long time, I felt somewhat alive.

"I'm free tomorrow night," I agreed. "Text me your address and pickup time before tomorrow, and I'll see you then."

"Okay," she breathed. Something in her voice made my body pull tight. I hung up, uncomfortable by the feeling, and yet exhilarated all the same. I sat the glass on the table and put the lid back on the bottle. I'm not quite sure if this is what Alex had in mind, but I'd taken up his advice. At least I was doing *something*.

Chapter 2

Clover

"And what would I have to do for the extra muffin?" Cassidy flirted with the entranced lunch boy. Despite my headache I couldn't help but smile. At least one of us was enjoying their day. She flicked back part of her honeycomb curls and toyed with her long dangly earrings. Her blue eyes danced with life over the younger lunch boy.

I'd been watching her through the glass walls of my office while trying to nullify this headache. I washed back another painkiller, downed my glass of water and pushed away from my desk. Manhattan was bustling behind me as it always did, morning and night. A delightful change from Ithaca, and yet I seemed to be missing my hometown more than I'd like to admit as of late.

I inevitably found myself peering over my shoulder at my busily typing boss, Debra Coorman. The source of all my anxieties and a real-life incarnation of *The Devil Wears Prada*. I'd sped through two years as her personal assistant at *Candice Magazine*, feeling like I only had daily migraines to show for it and no closer to becoming a travel columnist.

As if knowing I was looking her way, her green snake eyes landed on me. Her thin lips curled back, and she waved me into her office with exaggerated agitation. I sighed, frustrated that my glance alone invited her to beckon me like a dog. The packet of pain relief pills in my hand screamed at me to take one more tablet before I endured her company. Regretfully, I set them down and instead picked up my thin black reading glasses and placed them back over my eyes. I grabbed my current to-do list and grimaced at the state it was in.

She stroked through her mid-length brown hair, which had sharp red through it, much like her temper. The days of amicably working together were long gone after a few months of working here. One day she was fine and the next she was someone completely different. Since then, she'd been nothing but a bitch and acted like that was her full-time job too.

As I reached for the door handle, I caught sight of my watch. Time had slipped away and my advancing confrontation with Debra reassured me that I wouldn't finish alongside everyone else in the office in an hour's time.

"Clover," Debra snipped before I'd even fully opened the glass door that separated her office from mine. "I have a few more things for you to do this afternoon. I've compiled your list and sent it to your email. Also, your week of vacation leave has been denied for your requested dates. Perhaps a few weeks after that and you might have better luck."

"I put those dates in two months ago. It's that week specifically I need off for my sister's birthday," I replied calmly. I held back my annoyance because I knew it'd only make the situation worse.

"Well, unfortunately, Gary and I have organized a retreat for that weekend, so I need someone to run this place while I'm gone and to answer the clients' calls of course. You can always see your sister next year," she said spitefully, her arrogant composure inciting my anger even further. Of course she and her husband had organized a retreat that weekend. *How splendid for them,* I thought bitterly.

"Of course," I said with a reluctant smile. I kept my composure, knowing that it irked her even further. I still prided myself on my professionalism.

"This weekend we have the launch for our new contract with Issobelle Sherain. You out of all people should know how exciting it is for our magazine to have such a world-renowned photographer working for us."

Before I could even reply, she condescendingly continued as if I had no part onboarding her. "It's a significant gain for our magazine to now have Issobelle Sherain. And although she may be a young photographer, her photos are fantastic and quality. So much better since she moved from landscapes, in my opinion." I'd personally preferred her landscape images, but it was her *Short Boy* series that cemented her fame, and she was now hailed as the hip new artist of New York. She was considered a fresh breath in the world of photography and modeling and it was a shame she rarely posted landscapes ever since.

It *was* exciting for the team and magazine, but Debra's tone didn't convey that as she continued speaking.

"Because of this, we're gathering our sponsors and fellow chairmen across the board to acknowledge our efforts and personally welcome Issobelle with a party. I suspect our competitors won't be able to match us following this contract." Before I could interrupt her to remind her that I was the one who'd organized the event in the first place, she raised her hand to silence me. "You can now come."

"That's tomorrow night," I said, struggling to hide my irritation now. It was bad enough when she daringly excluded me from the party. But now to last-minute invite me? That left almost no time for preparation. I was certain she was trying to humiliate me in front of the board members.

"Correct," she said contemplatively. "Also, Geesh is still ill and can't update the website with our new exposure on Issobelle. I need you to deal with that. Upon agreement with Issobelle, we'll also have direct links to her individual website. We need to create a webpage for her that merges her look with ours as a united front. I need that updated by Sunday. Don't forget your list either."

"Sunday? That's the day after the campaign, which is only tomorrow night." I took a deep breath, imploring patience. "And, I know nothing about website design."

"Clover, I can't have this be a disappointment. If you can't do it, I'll simply find someone else who

Kia Carrington-Russell

can," she said snidely. It wasn't the first time she'd threatened my job. "It can only be updated the night before, so good luck. I expect to see a fully working release page on it by midnight Saturday. Also, while you're on your way out, can you grab a coffee from the lunch boy for me before he starts licking Cassidy's face." She issued me a light, fake smile.

My mind raced through all the venomous things I wanted to call her. I bit my words back. I couldn't let her bullying risk me imploding and tarnishing my name within the industry, and yet my mind boggled over interesting names and replies.

"Clover, you do have a boyfriend now, don't you? What are you, twenty-eight? Cassidy mentioned to me you have a boyfriend which is a relief because I was starting to worry about you. I thought, for some reason, men didn't have much of an attraction toward you. But now with a boyfriend in the picture, I can relax. I have no doubt he must be very handsome." She let the bitter words hang in the air. "I look forward to meeting him tomorrow night."

My composure was left intact. I'd learned to mask my agitation when people pried into my love life or commented on my appearance, especially in this spiteful way. I didn't deem myself anything spectacular in appearance, but with Latino curves

10

that my mother had learnt to embrace, I found myself subconscious as some women judged me around their husbands and men couldn't keep their gaze on my eyes. My sister, Megan always joked, *jealousy is a curse* but it made me want to hide even further.

The small to-do list crumpled in my hand as I walked out. I wasn't looking forward to what would be waiting in my emails to replace it. I straightened my pencil skirt over my hips, trying to summon some semblance of calm. I didn't have the slightest clue how to create a new website page. I didn't even know where to start. And despite my pounding headache, I needed a coffee to get me through the rest of the afternoon.

"Ah, Clover," Cassidy cheered excitedly when I walked over to her.

"Hey," I acknowledged her glumly. "Darrel, can you please take a cappuccino, one and a half sugars, lukewarm, to Mrs. Coorman." He left with a bounce in his step. Cassidy waved him away with a lingering smile as she slid over my already made latte to me. Looking at the clock on the wall while rubbing my neck and shoulders, I knew I wouldn't be getting out at the same time as everyone else.

"You didn't mention to Debra that I had a

boyfriend, did you?" I asked, although I already doubted it.

"No, why? Do you?" Cassidy asked almost affronted by the thought of not being told.

"No. She wants me to go to the party tomorrow night with only a day's notice. Because of the work-load she just dumped on me, I don't even have time to buy a dress for it. She even decided to throw in a snipe about me not having a boyfriend or date at the previous campaigns." I rubbed my forehead in frustration. The bitter dislike I held toward her was small in comparison to the workload she'd just burdened me with.

"Well, you can look at my dresses," she replied excitedly. I assessed her size against my own. She was always racing through fad diets and dropping weight for boys she'd liked. I guessed I was easily an extra twenty pounds heavier than her. Before I could argue, she added, "I could even do your hair. I have a few accessories that will bring out your coloring, and I have the nicest green shades that will highlight your brown eyes. Oh, and I just learned this new trick from YouTube, you're going to love it."

"I don't even have a mask," I argued. Why had I thought a masquerade ball was a good idea?

"I have three you can choose from," Cassidy

added with a polite smile, purposefully cutting down my excuses.

I wanted to curl up on her desk and just give up on the task at hand. Cassidy had always looked stunning on nights of events though, I just wasn't sure if her style necessarily translated into my own. Whatever that was these days. And I didn't have much choice either. I politely added, "Thank you."

"So, what are you going to do about the boyfriend thing?" Cassidy asked, breaking me out of my inner pity-party.

"I don't know. I haven't been on a date for as long as I can remember."

"But surely, you've made some guy friends who can help you out?"

Sheepishly, I folded into myself. I didn't know how to put nicely that I hadn't made any friends since moving to the city. My focus had purely been on work, but I didn't want to throw a sticker on my forehead that said *has no friends* either. "I haven't really met anyone since I've moved here." I glumly sighed and quietly admitted to myself. "I can't even think of anyone to ask to escort me."

"That's it!" Cassidy exclaimed, startling me. She rummaged through her bag. After a fruitless struggle with an invisible animal that seemed to strangle her hand from the depths of the big bottomless pit she called her bag, she emptied the contents onto her desk. Bright lipsticks, perfumes, and jewelry littered the table.

"Do you have half of your apartment in there?" I asked, amazed.

"Ha. Ha," she replied as she flicked through the small purple purse. I contemplated whether a kitchen sink could fit as well. She scanned through its insides before fixating on a card and with triumph, offered it to me. "His name is Damon, and he offers an hourly rate."

"An hourly rate?" I looked at the card with suspicion. "Cassidy... this is an escort's card," I said cautiously, wondering if she knew what "his services" actually entailed.

"I know isn't it exciting!" She bounced. "One of my friends gave me the card. And ironically, he only does masquerade balls, but she said he was great and utterly divine and you could tell even through the mask that he was *superhot*. She even showed me a photo! At least this way you won't rock up by yourself. His charm and looks will make *her* even more envious. And it's completely confidential, so no one will know." She flicked her bouncy curls over her shoulder and looked around to make sure no one was listening. "What's there to lose?"

"My pride, dignity, respect?"

"Oh stop being so dramatic. People need to make their living somehow and if you're hot why not exploit it," she said with a hand on her hip.

As if secrecy were contagious, I glanced around before looking at the card again. "I'm not sure about this. It makes me feel pathetic that I can't find a date myself. And besides, what's so wrong with being single and independent? That was always something I was proud of. Until today," I added glumly. I looked down at the simple black card. The gold calligraphy was elegant and tasteful. It cited only a first name, a contact number, and the most important word of all. *Escort*.

"You're not a loser for using someone's services. It's a business transaction. And there's nothing wrong with being single and proud. But just this once, wouldn't it be fun to see her expression when you turn up with your 'boyfriend.' She'll be so jealous. Gary doesn't have much to offer in the looks department anymore." She laughed lightly. "Let your hair out once, Clover. Dance with the devil a little."

I frowned at her, offering an effective expression that had her raising her arms in defense. "It's just a suggestion. Live a little, Clover. You deserve to have fun sometimes too."

I fiddled with the card in my hand, and as I did, a more immature part of me acknowledged how great it would be to trump Debra just this once. I couldn't help but consider it. "Maybe," I pondered, walking back to my office to face the dreaded to-do list.

Hours later, I was alone in the office and still busily replying to clients and sponsors. Every time I unearthed a new set of instructions highlighting another unrealistic task, I fought the urge to reach for the phone. I looked from the chic black card to the time: 10:00 p.m. I froze as once again my fingers itched to call the number. *His* number. Just this once, I wanted to see an expression of embarrassed repentance fleet across Debra's sharp features. Especially now that I was buried in so much work. But as quickly as my hand stretched out toward my phone, it retreated with the unsettling feeling of the unknown.

I sighed to myself and fixated on the framed photo of me and my sister beside my desk. It was a constant reminder of the promise I'd made to her before moving here. That I would make something of myself and look after our family. Megan and I didn't really look the same. I was brunette and curvaceous. She was athletic and blonde. We were so different and part of me was always envious of her light-hearted spirit, especially when I missed it now. I looked at my phone again, and much like Cassidy she would've encouraged the spark of a new adventure. And she'd always had the most outrageous and exciting stories to be told.

I picked up my phone again, trying my best to embody that confidence and thrill. But I found that I couldn't force my fingers to dial the number and sent a simple text instead. *Is this Damon?* Instantly, I set the phone down almost it'd scorched me. I studied my list once again as if it would be enough to hide me from what I'd just done.

The sudden vibration and glow of my phone jolted me back upright. I stared at it. The number I'd just text was calling me. I didn't think he would respond so quickly. My heart pounded and I ignored my reluctance to answer the phone. I knew Megan would be cheering me on. *Do something fun, maybe even risky,* she'd joke.

I answered the phone.

"Hello?" I said shakily, feeling stupid.

"Do you need to be escorted somewhere?" a low, deep voice asked.

"Um." I was surprised by the enticing voice on the other end. How long had I been gaping silently at my phone. I cleared my throat. If he looked as sexy as he sounded, then he would be perfect to show Debra up. This was business. "I do. It's a... a formal event.

"I only do masquerade."

"It is masquerade," I blurted out. "Tomorrow night?"

There was a long pause. Was it because I didn't sound the part? Or did he have to move other clients around? How many clients did this guy even have?

"I'm free tomorrow night," he said smoothly. "Text me your address and pickup time before tomorrow, and I'll see you then."

"Okay," I agreed breathlessly, almost shocked by my immediate submission.

And then he hung up. I felt like I'd committed a crime. But I had to admit, the secrecy of it was exciting. Thrilling even. I looked at the photo of Megan and started smiling at the thought of what she would say. Much like Cassidy, I think she'd agree that getting an escort to annoy Debra was a daring way to stand up for myself.

I texted Damon my address and time of pickup and then refocused on my work, suddenly with all the exhilarated energy in the world. I'd make a good impression tomorrow at the party. I wouldn't let Debra look down on me any longer. This was one of her games I was willing to play for the first time. I accepted the challenge.

Chapter 3

Clover

At 2:00 a.m. the bustling city was no quieter, but my gaze and body sagged with exhaustion. My headache had only worsened and when I began to see small black dots, I decided it was time to call it a night. I'd been managing multiple clients, ensuring their confidence in our ad space as many recently deferred to our top competitor, *Be True* magazine. And I had no doubt that when they read that email, they too would be thinking, "why are you even up at this time?"

I had no choice but to leave the website design until tomorrow. Exhaustedly, I gathered my books and bags before turning all the lights off. I stopped turning them off when Lucy, the cleaning lady, ventured in with a large trolley of cleaning products. "Is she working you to the bone again, Miss Granture?" Lucy asked with a crooked smile. I gave her a soft one in return.

"Oh, how too often we meet like this," I responded sleepily, reflecting on how often I was in the office so late. "Have a good morning, Lucy."

I waited patiently in the lift for the doors to close while clutching my handbag, work bag, and balancing all my files. The cheery notes of the elevator music taunted my already taut nerves. Pressing my back against the metal bar behind me, I peered up at the mirrored roof. Black bags were etched under my eyes and my figure sagged with fatigue. And yet that jolt of disbelieving energy passed through my body the moment I thought about the phone call that had been made.

Tightening my scarf around my neck, I braced myself for the cool breeze of the autumn night air. Immediately my breath pillowed in soft puffs. The air was unusually icy for this early in fall. I held my arm out to a passing taxi, which thankfully screeched to a halt.

I blinked tiredly at the *Candice* building as we pulled away and merged with the traffic. To others it probably looked just as formidable. It was stark and intimidating—perfect for a high-end fashion magazine.

The taxi crawled behind some cars leading to a set of lights, and, glancing past my tired reflection, I saw a locked magazine stand on the sidewalk. Through the metal bars I could just make out our rival magazine glistening with gold text. It was the new issue of the monthly magazine. For many years I had my eye on *Be True* magazine. The difference between their magazine and ours was far too obvious at times, not only in sales but in style and content as well. Currently, they had the critically-acclaimed ballerina, Sarah Hine, on their cover. She'd quickly denied our request for a photoshoot with her, I now understood why.

I had to disown my interest in their magazine a long time ago. Sometimes, in an act of petty revenge, I would buy a copy here and there to read my favorite article by the celebrated writer known as Anonymous. Her writing was magnificent, and she conveyed fantastic stories on any topic she covered, including travel, which I so enviously wanted to write myself. I envied Anonymous for having such powers of expression and for the freedom to write whatever it was that took her fancy. Her writing had such a sensitive and rich tone, and she was appreciative of culture and nature, all while being a quiet authority on fashion and style. My goal was to reach the same level of fame, not just for recognition, but for the liberty to express myself freely and pay my bills by doing it.

Watching the city lights while being driven to my apartment, I observed the couples who walked together in the late night, arm in arm. Was it sad that I hadn't yet attempted to date any men since moving here? I had no reason to be repulsed by men. I'd never been scorned. My flings only lasted a short time before I became annoyed by their immaturity and lack of ambition. The longest relationship I had lasted no more than six months, and that was back in Ithaca. It had only made me more reluctant to date the men of Manhattan. Weren't they all more or less the same? But if I was being honest with myself, the concept of having a boyfriend or even a lover now seemed foreign because I only had time for work.

I stared at my phone, wishing it would glow with a personal message or a missed call, something to validate that someone needed me outside *Candice*. I opened it, rereading my two messages to the escort. How unlike me to message him on a whim.

My curiosity piqued. I wondered who he was. I tried to picture a face to match the voice as I replayed his voice in my mind, his husky tone a satisfying vibration down my spine. I furrowed my eyebrows, recalling I hadn't asked how much his... escorting... would cost. Was it inappropriate to ask an escort, "How much?" It's not like he was a prostitute. I blushed at the thought and hid the phone away as if it contained my dirty little thoughts and secret.

I paid the cab driver, thanking him before waiting for the elevator to reach level nine in my building. It was a sparse and barely decorated hallway with terrible, flaking blue walls but it was manageable on my wage. I leaned against the wall as I fumbled inside my bags for the key to my apartment.

When I finally stepped inside, I was greeted by Pudding, my ginger cat that I'd owned since I was sixteen. He rubbed my leg impatiently. He'd gone all day and night without food.

"I'm sorry, Pudding!" I bumped my hip against the front door to close it before he tried to make his grand escape.

Guilt drove me forward, and I hurriedly dumped my bags on my dining table. In his impatience, he'd knocked over my large blue vase that lovingly housed a fake plant. "Ahh, why?" I asked, thankful he hadn't broken it. I set it upright once again in the corner of my dining room, fluffing the artificial purple flowers in it before quickly feeding the few fish in the tank behind the dining table.

I tiredly walked into the kitchen and rummaged through the high cupboard near my fridge. Pudding impatiently rubbed against my legs again as I opened the can. He dragged one nail down my hosiery splitting it, probably in spite for not feeding him sooner. "Ah, Pudding," I whined at the malicious cat. Dishing out some canned food, I began to mix it with the dry biscuits, but he shouldered me out of the way. I gave up on the battle when he began downing his food. "You're such a determined thing," I hissed, thinking of the cat-dominating-the-world scenario I sometimes saw in films. If any cat could, it would be Pudding.

I threw my ruined hosiery at the bin, missing miserably—they could stay there for the time being, I didn't have the energy to pick them up. I contemplated a shower and immediately lost any intention I had of it when my eyes fell upon my comfy blue couch in my lounge room, with the bright lights of the city dazzling behind.

I caught sight of my bedroom as I collapsed on the couch. It looked gloomy and dark. There was a pile of washing that still had to be ironed and folded.

I'll get to that tomorrow, I convinced myself, covering my face with my arm and removing my reading glasses that I'd almost forgotten I still had on. "I am absolutely exhausted," I yawned to myself, snuggling into the couch and almost immediately falling into the welcome respite of deep sleep.

Startled by a banging noise, I sat upright and rubbed my eyes. When lucid, I realized someone was knocking on my door. I patted down my hair and wiped away the drool as I staggered to the door, still disoriented and exhausted.

"Good afternoon," Cassidy chirped as she took a step back and assessed me as if I was some barbaric cavewoman. Her hair was pinned into a messy bun on top of her head, and she was clad in casual sweat-pants and a warm coat. She held out a few silver garment bags and a large makeup case. "You obviously weren't prepared for my arrival," she laughed as she walked in and greeted Pudding. "Ooh you have a cat! And here I thought you could hardly look after yourself."

"Ha. Ha. Wait, did you say afternoon?" I replied

and was shocked at the time on my silver wristwatch. It was already past midday. "Shit, I didn't realize it was so late already," I panicked as I looked at my desk in horror. I hadn't done any research on how to create a webpage. I hadn't even checked my emails.

"You obviously needed the sleep. What time did you get home last night?" Cassidy asked, placing the dresses over the sofa and pulling things out of her makeup case.

"No, I don't have time to sleep," I mumbled, turning on my laptop. I only had a few hours until I had to leave for the campaign. My stomach immediately blossomed with butterflies in anticipation of the person I'd be going with. *I didn't have time to worry about that.*

"Leave that for now, you're a smart cookie. You'll be able to do that tonight or you can give her the middle finger." I gave Cassidy an effective glance, and she laughed. "Let me do this for you first. I have a date soon so I can't be here all afternoon," she beamed.

I was conflicted. I wanted her help, but I needed to do research. This was exactly what Debra wanted. But then again, if I didn't look the part, I was equally a failure in her eyes. I relented. I could do the work after Cassidy left. *Just a few copy and pastes here and there. Easy*, I deluded myself.

"I wasn't too sure, so I brought a red dress and a green dress. I think the green will look nicer on you and fit your curves better as well. But it doesn't hurt to have options. But first, I'm going to let you shower before you put on my dress," Cassidy chimed. I looked over myself, embarrassed that I was still wearing my work clothes from yesterday.

"A shower sounds good," I agreed.

Enjoying the brief shower, I breathed in the steamy air, trying to wake myself. I still couldn't believe I'd slept for so long. I stepped out, quickly wiping over myself before walking out in my towel and immediately gunned for the coffee machine.

Cassidy was playing with Pudding. A small feather attached to her necklace captured his attention, much to Cassidy's delight. Sensing her enthusiasm for the game, he began to ignore it, and only flicked it out of his way a few more times out of annoyance. "I love your Pudding. He's so much fun," Cassidy said, smitten. "Now, try the green one. I think it's a better shade for your hair." She gestured to the dress.

"I really don't mind which one," I politely said. "As long as I look presentable, I won't have to deal with yet another awkward conversation with Debra about my 'lazy attire.' Despite how glamorous I may look I'm sure she'll still point out my many faults."

"Maybe she'll drink too much bubbles and make a fool of herself. Wouldn't that be a sight to behold," she laughed to herself, comfortably perched across my couch. "Oh and I brought you two different masks to try on. The third was bright pink and I didn't think it was your style, really."

I dreaded the thought of a pink mask. After a mouthful of my hazelnut coffee, I attempted to squeeze into the green dress. "Cassidy, I really don't think this will fit me," I admitted.

"Anyone can fit into this one," she dismissed. I sucked in, and to my surprise, she was able to zip it halfway up my back. "It's easy." She firmly pinched her fingers around the zip so she could fully enclose my frame into the tight-fitting dress. I exasperatedly exhaled as the material finally entrapped me before taking a few unsure steps.

"There's no way I could move in this," I said, trying to adjust my stance and straighten my back so walking was less awkward.

"It looks amazing on you. Some simple black heels will go perfectly with it."

Cassidy played with her hair behind me as I

turned back and forth staring into my full-length mirror in the living room trying to get used to the feel of the tight material over my body. The dress felt oh-so-tight, but it clung to my figure beautifully. My stomach was slim, and my curves were perfectly in proportion. This wasn't a dress, it was some kind of magical body suit. I forced my gaze away from the mirror to my silver wristwatch. Time was already slipping through my grasp.

"Okay, now don't even think of taking that off, because, well, I don't know if we can get you back in it." She laughed to herself. "Now, let me do your hair and makeup."

We moved into the bathroom to continue the makeover. I could've done it myself, but she seemed to be enjoying it far too much for me to deny her the pleasure. Quickly, she proved she was rather talented at it. She applied smoky shades to my eyes and a deep brown to my lips. She curled my hair and loosely pinned it into a bun, almost knocking me unconscious with the amount of hairspray she added. I was almost crawling out of the bathroom to escape it. But she assured me the more the better, even after I told her my hair held curls because of its natural wave. But trying to convince the determined Cassidy was a mission on its own.

A dark-green mask proved to match the dress. It felt like I was an entirely different person and a part of me liked the magic of it. I shuffled around my house afterward, holding my hands to my stomach as I embraced the tightness of the dress, waving goodbye to the chance of eating anything that evening. Cassidy received a call and quickly approved my appearance before fluttering away to her date. She left her belongings at mine, claiming she would pick them up later.

I felt like I was on a mission as soon as she shut the door behind her. I logged onto my laptop, allowing my mind to wallow in the research about webpages while scanning over numerous forums. Okay, time to start the impossible task of having to complete this overnight.

Entranced by my work, a knock on my door promptly scattered my thoughts. I jumped out of the chair, noticing it was already six. The escort was here. I'd lost track of time—again.

Chapter 4

Clover

"In a minute," I called shakily, surprised by my nerves. I hurriedly slipped on my black heels and checked myself over once again in the full-length mirror in my living room. I thought I looked good, not that I was trying to impress him. This was, of course, business- pure and simple- yet my heart still raced in excitement. I threw my brown lipstick and apartment keys into my black sparkly clutch. I saved the work on my laptop and then patted Pudding's head before racing for the door. I opened it in a hurry, catching my clutch on the door and hooking myself. I scrambled to pick it up before drinking in the man standing in front of me.

My lips went thin. I suppressed the urge to say anything at all in case I mumbled some incomprehensible nonsense. I stood there for a moment, dumbfounded by his attractiveness even hidden away by a mask. There was only so much a mask could hide, and prominent cheekbones, molten brown eyes, lush lips, trimmed facial hair with an effortless tan was not left to the imagination. It wasn't just his looks. He had an undeniable presence. Confidence emanated from him.

He might've been only a few years older than me but younger than what his deep voice would suggest. Or maybe he was younger than me I realized? How would I ever know? Butterflies scattered in my stomach. His dark-brown hair was nicely slicked back, just touching his collar. Even his jaw was perfectly chiseled and strong. And he smelled so *good*.

"Clover, I assume?" His lip twisted into a courteous smile and handed me a red rose. I searched those dark, molten eyes that seemed to stare straight into my very being. One hand was casually placed in his pocket, which just pulled his black suit enough for me to get an impression of the body behind the smart shirt. My eyes lingered on the belt at his waist. Catching myself and embarrassed, I caught his gaze again. *Down, Clover, it hasn't been that long since you've been so close to a man.*

"Ah, yes, that's me," I said stupidly, wanting to slap myself.

I straightened as if I were giving a presentation in front of an intimidating client. *Get a hold of yourself, anyone would assume you haven't seen a man your whole life,* I chastised internally. I collected myself with a confidence I didn't feel. *This is just business.*

I accepted the red rose with a curt smile. "And you're Damon, I presume?"

"It depends on how many other escorts you've hired for the night called Damon?" I blushed, looking down the hallway to make sure no one heard. His smile grew and I was shell-shocked. Was he... *teasing* me? "I believe we have somewhere to be?"

He offered his elbow out to me, gentlemanlike. I hesitated to take it, feeling that this was all slightly over the top. No one ever offered their elbow to a woman these days. Or did they? *When was the last time I dated that guy... what was his name... Jimmy?* I hauled myself back to reality. I was paying for this, so I might as well enjoy it.

"So where are we heading then?" he asked amiably as we headed for the elevator.

I assessed him from the side, almost brooding at the realization that even his side profile was just as stunning. I felt like someone had suddenly thrown me onto the arm of a celebrity and I'd forgotten how to converse like a normal human. I slapped myself internally again. I'd dealt with big clients all the time and I had to treat this no differently. *This was business.* "The *Candice Magazine* campaign. It's the opening for Issobelle Sherain, in celebration of her recruitment and exclusivity. We'll greet the sponsors, hear some speeches, that kind of thing." By talking about work, I began to relax a little. My heart no longer raced as speedily as before.

"You work for the *Candice Magazine*?" Damon asked curiously, looking past his shoulder because of our height difference.

"I'm the personal assistant to the CEO there. Also, I'm sorry to have asked you to escort me at such late notice. I wasn't expecting to go until the last minute and I had no time to organize a partner," I said, trying to play it casually. It was partly true, at least. But I'd have to tell him because in the likely event Debra would interrogate him about our relationship, I'd need him to lie for me. "Actually..." I stopped in front of the elevator, drawing us both to a halt. "I know this is going to sound pathetic, but my boss has been giving me a really hard time, and usually I wouldn't play these games, but I somehow got ensnared. She... may have mocked me for not having a partner, and somehow manipulated me into thinking I needed to prove her wrong, and so I ended up calling you. And... I really don't even know what I'm doing right now," I ranted, realizing how utterly embarrassing the situation was and just how juvenile I must sound.

"So, you want me to pretend to be your boyfriend for the night so that it somehow feels like a win against your boss?" Another smile blossomed, displaying his perfectly white teeth.

I looked away not allowing myself to fall for that dazzling smile that undoubtedly many women had fallen for. With far too much confidence I replied, "Basically."

He pushed the button for the elevator before looking at me with a calm smile and reverence. "Okay, I can do that. Although I must admit, it's the first job I've had under these kinds of circumstances. I don't know if I should be flattered or wary of you," he said jokingly before stepping into the elevator when the doors finally opened. I felt red heat my cheeks. *Wary of me?* "Are you coming?"

"It's completely transactional of course," I blurted out before I squeezed beside him in the small elevator. A small chuckle rumbled through him, heating my cheeks further. His cologne was powerful and masculine. *Expensive tastes*, I noted approvingly. I couldn't help but shoot him a glance as we stood together, unsure how to take him or the situation. He was so charming at my door, and yet he teased me about my situation, slightly putting me at ease. He could've pronounced me weird, or outright told me "no." But instead he took the situation in good humor. There was a sense of playfulness behind his suave smile. It was a winning combination for which I was sure he was highly paid.

"So, do we do pet names?" he asked casually, placing his hands into the pockets of his expensive-looking pants.

"Definitely not," I snapped, surprised at my quick opposition. He gave an even smile at my reaction without saying anything in response.

He ushered me out of the building and stepped onto the road to flag a taxi. Suddenly I was aware of the other people on the busy sidewalk. Women stumbled as they passed him, and men shot him looks of surprised envy. Some teenage girls giggled obviously as they passed him. I blushed on his behalf. I wondered if they would think I wasn't good enough for him. I looked down at my black clutch self-consciously.

Well, he isn't my man. I am paying for him to escort me, I reminded myself. *So, tonight, I'm good enough.*

I looked at him in a new light. He was indeed my trump card and I would make the most of his services tonight.

Chapter 5

Damon

Clover shifted uncomfortably in the back of the taxi, seeming unsure as to what to do with her hands. We sat in a companionable silence, but I could tell already she wasn't a woman who got unnerved too often. And when she did, it appeared she didn't know how to hold herself.

She was the embodiment of beautiful, even masked; I imagined men dropped to her feet hoping she'd give them the time of day. Beautiful smooth skin that I could almost imagine the texture of in my palm and curves that seemed to scream under the binding of that tight dress—one that I appreciated the sight of. It was a mystery how a woman such as this couldn't obtain a date, even last minute in Manhattan.

"You're legal age, aren't you?"

My eyebrows shot up in surprise. "What?"

"You're not like a twenty-year-old with an impeccable beard, are you? You can legally drink and stuff, right?"

I had to turn my face away and laugh silently to myself, hoping that she wouldn't hear it.

"Why are you laughing?" she reprimanded, covering her own embarrassment.

I faced her, still delightfully smiling. "You do realize, it's rude to ask an escort their age, right?"

Her shoulders sagged and a frown marred her flawless skin. "Oh."

Again, I chuckled to myself. Well, there was a first for everything I supposed. "I'm thirty-two."

"Okay, that's good to know," she admitted. Her whitening knuckles around the clutch seemed to receive some blood flow again. "Have you been doing this long?"

"This?" I teased, gratified when she went into another blubbering spiral.

"This... career path of yours..."

I chuckled, unable not to laugh at her. It was endearing in a way. She was a rare species in Manhattan indeed.

"I'm new to this kind of thing okay, so I'm sorry if

my questions are laughable," she flushed with a temper, sparking my interest even more.

"I'm sorry, it's just refreshing."

"What is?"

"You," I said. "I haven't met a woman like you before." Yes, I'd met women who fawned over me. Some who couldn't even articulate a word when I walked into a room. But this was... different. But despite my intended compliment, she seemed to take offence. She silently faced the window.

Before I could apologize, she seemed to find more interest in her phone as she scanned through webpages. I didn't consider myself much of a snoop, but I was curious as to what could be so important when she was paying for my time and decidedly ignored me instead. I was almost wounded by the lack of attention.

Static crackled through the taxi, and we both looked up. The radio had lost signal. The driver mumbled something incomprehensible before hitting the "off" button. Immediately, we were immersed in awkward silence. I took advantage of the diversion. "Do you write yourself?" I asked. It was safe to assume most who worked at a fashion magazine usually didn't want to stop at only being a personal assistant.

She seemed torn as to whether to reply or continue her research on what looked to be website design. The cab driver seemed to be watching us through the mirror, sitting in awkward silence.

"Partially," she answered animatedly. "For the time being, I'm a little tied up and can't find the time to write. But I've written all my life."

"What kind of pieces did you start with?" I asked, trying to keep the conversation flowing. I didn't want her feeling uncomfortable by my presence. Most women I'd spent time with often filled the space with things they liked, ambitions, how they stumbled into Manhattan. But Clover... she was different. This seemed to very much be a business transaction for her. And I was often used to woman fawning over me when I stepped into this role. I almost *wanted* and *demanded* her attention.

"It was only short stories and articles as a freelancer at the start. Eventually, I did become a journalist for two years in Ithaca for the local newspaper. I quit that a couple of years ago and moved to Manhattan hoping to become a travel columnist, ironically." She seemed almost deflated.

"Why ironically?" I encouraged. That strong, honey gaze of hers pierced me. There was a wariness to her. And it wasn't simply because she wore a mask. Now I was even more curious as to what she might look like beneath.

"Because I couldn't be further away from that goal right now."

"Because of your tyrant boss?" I asked.

Silence. She nibbled at her bottom lip as though I'd just struck a nerve. She was cautious, wary of me even and how much she wanted to share. I decided to tread carefully. "Why travel journalism, then?"

Her eyes lit up, her passion inciting something that I found rather alluring. "I want to write pieces on the world—on culture, life, and traditions. New York is the furthest I've got to reaching that goal," she finished dejectedly. She hadn't traveled, despite wanting to be a travel journalist? Before I could interject, she quickly perked up. "It'll happen. I'm optimistic and working myself to the bone to make it happen."

I deliberated on how I should phrase my next question. If she wanted to explore the world so badly, then why did she confine herself in a job where her boss played malicious games. "Then why do you work a job that you feel isn't getting you anywhere?"

Again, she seemed surprised by my question. Perhaps she was expecting me to be nothing but pretty. A toy she could show off tonight. And although I was more than happy to oblige, I found myself curious about this woman who hid behind more than her masquerade mask. She clutched at the silver necklace at her breasts, my gaze inevitably dropping before I looked away and shifted uncomfortably.

Her tone had changed, becoming one of dealing with a client, seeming more smooth and polished. Distant from everything else her body was telling me. *She was uncertain.* "I never said it wasn't going anywhere. I'm happy where I am now. I like my job, although not my boss. But, it keeps me on my toes and challenges me. It affords me one step toward the direction I want to go in, and I'm sure another will soon come if I work hard enough," she said, somewhat defensively. "How did you become an escort?" Her tone lacked tact, no doubt evening the score for my personal question.

"This night isn't about me; it's about you, Clover," I dismissed her question smoothly.

"Do most women enjoy your company? I apologize if I'm forward, but I've never been escorted. Is it your job to act like this in front of those who you're trying to impress, as well as me?"

I was taken back by her accusation and crossed

my arms over my chest, filling the space. I studied her for a moment, my finger pressed against my lips thoughtfully. "Who said I was acting?" I offered a coy smile, trying to de-escalate the intense mood the cab had now taken.

"Your eyes," she simply said. I warily studied her. No one saw through my masks, only when I wanted them too. She looked at her phone again and said, "Checkmate."

My face scrunched up in confused bewilderment. "Why did you 'checkmate' me?"

"It's uncomfortable when someone assumes that they know you isn't it?" That honey gaze struck me with a formidable intellect. When was the last time someone spoke to me like this? Only my sister had ever dared to challenge me so forwardly. "You might as well be yourself. I certainly won't paint a pretty picture of who I am over the next few hours. In fact, you probably will be begging me to go home early so you don't have to put up with me anymore," she laughed as she began scrolling through her phone again. And just like that, the nervous woman was gone, replaced by this fiery woman who'd suddenly left me unable to respond.

My mouth opened but nothing came out. Had

my charm... failed? She shot me a knowing sideways glance, as if permitting that I could now speak to her.

A coy smile spread over both our lips, almost contagious. I liked this woman, she held her own without remorse or apology. "It's easy to talk to you," I admitted.

The cab driver and I exchanged an interesting glance through the rearview mirror.

"Wait until I've had a few wines, you'll be sick of me yet. I haven't drunk in a while," she brushed off my comment lightly. Her gaze dropped unable to match my own. "Have you been to a campaign like this before?"

"I've been to one or two. I get the gist of how it works—a few speeches of thanks, food, champagne, and more champagne. Don't worry, I'll make a good impression." Because I always had to. It was what I was raised for.

"Okay, well, thank you then," she replied. Lights streaked her face as streetlamps illuminated well-cared-for stores and the manicured trees that lined the boulevards of Lower Manhattan.

The taxi was slowing as we'd arrived at our destination. The building was tall and brightly lit. Clover handed the taxi driver money. I rounded the car and opened her door, offering my hand in a gentlemanly manner. "Are you ready for this, Clover?"

"I have no choice now," she smiled. And our little charade began. I was right to answer her call. After all, this would be an exciting evening and this dazzling woman was undoubtedly about to stir a lot of fun.

Chapter 6

Clover

Young men in white suits and masks greeted guests at the door with champagne. I noticed a few familiar sponsors I'd met previously. The masks however did hinder recognizing everyone. Some had their faces completely covered in a fashionable statement and others modest with a simpler touch.

I inhaled deeply, breathing in confidence; walking into such large glittering events still seemed intimidating at times and I'd learnt that shoulders back and head high was always a great start. I greeted the doorman and walked through the glass doors, hips swaying confidently. It was time to play *my* part.

We walked through the hall and into a ballroom. Soft music played, and guests talked with one another in high spirits. Bright glass chandeliers were hanging from the ceiling and a large open space for dancing was in the middle of the room. On the stage was a small lively band playing jazz music. The four members were evidently comfortable as they passionately played. Directly across from us was the buffet, and on the right, a small crowd had formed around Issobelle Sherain, congratulating her. I only recognized her amongst the crowd by the lopsided edgy blue bob cut, because her flamingo mask was an outstanding sight to behold.

Flashes from a cameraman taking photos grabbed my attention. When he spotted us, the young man walked over, nibbling at the toothpick in his mouth. "Smile," he instructed, aiming the camera at us. Damon placed his hand around my waist, catching me off guard with a touch I hadn't felt for years. His cologne lingered in the air as I looked up at him, surprised by his quick dominance of the situation. He was smiling toward the camera, and I saw that the cameraman was patiently waiting for me to look his way too. I smiled, feeling a hot flush across my cheeks.

"Yep, it's good," the cameraman said, giving us the thumbs-up before walking away.

"You're quick to cling to the hips," I said jokingly as I peeled myself from his hold.

"Your dress feels tight," he whispered. I flushed red in embarrassment, giving him the satisfaction he was obviously after.

Before I could say anything witty in response, I noticed Debra and her husband, Gary, coming toward us from the corner of my eye. A waiter walked past me, and I quickly collected one of the glasses of red wine from the tray, gulping a mouthful.

"Clover, how nice that you could make it," Debra said brightly, looking over Damon like a cougar eyeing her prey. I was disgusted to think of all the things that might've been rolling around in her mind. Subtlety was never her strength. "And who is your friend?"

"I'm Damon, and I assume you're Debra?" Damon smiled cunningly as he glanced my way, as if in confirmation.

I took another mouthful of my wine, hoping that it would quickly ease the discomfort of being in her presence. I was impressed though, he'd been polite to her, but his eyes were still on me.

"Oh, you've heard of me?" she asked flirtatiously.

Gary seemed unfazed by his wife's intentions. Perhaps he was used to it. "Clover, how have you been? I haven't seen you around for a while," Gary said, ignoring Damon and Debra's conversation. Gary always held a gaze that would never break; its intensity I found uncomfortable at first. But after a few events and conversations I realized he was a nice enough man, very different from his wife. I always considered it kind of him to make the effort to converse with me at these events, unlike Debra who often tried to embarrass me one way or another.

"Of course I've heard of you," Damon said charismatically. Then, almost abruptly, he turned his attention to Gary. He offered him his hand. "And you are?"

The atmosphere suddenly became prickly as Gary looked between me and Damon's extended hand. He seemed hesitant to accept it, which I found surprising. Gary reached out for it under Debra's pressuring gaze.

"I'm Gary," he said awkwardly as they shook hands. Gary looked at me again before quickly diverting his gaze elsewhere, which was also very unlike him. *Strange.* Debra scowled at me as if I'd been the one to personally make her husband uncomfortable. Damon wrapped his hand around my shoulder possessively, no doubt looking the part.

I wasn't sure what was going on, but it wasn't pleasant for any of us.

"So, Clover's spoken of me?" Debra prompted again, dismissing her husband.

Gary burned holes at Damon's hand around my shoulder before finding interest with some nearby sponsors. I thought Damon was meant to schmooze and charm everyone over, not create enemies with the boss's husband who I was already having issues with.

It also irked me more than feeling triumphant that Debra would so quickly flirt with someone I claimed to be my boyfriend. And it was evidently making her husband just as uncomfortable—though two minutes ago he seemed fine.

"All good things, of course, isn't that right, my little muffin?" Damon smirked.

My left eye twitched in response. We'd agreed to no pet names. He *was* teasing me. My temper flared. This guy had no idea who was dealing with. Paid services be damned, I wasn't going to be teased all night and stand for it.

I offered my most insufferable doting smile. "Of course, my love pet," I said, a hint of annoyance edging my voice. Damon pressed his head behind mine, covering the small chuckle that he was fighting back so Debra wouldn't see.

Debra looked at me, unimpressed with my familiarity with her new toy. She smiled once again at Damon. "How did you two meet?" she asked.

I paled. Oh shit. We hadn't thought this far. How had I forgotten this part? We should've been discussing it in the cab.

"It's actually a pretty embarrassing story on my behalf," Damon answered, pulling me in closer his hand comfortably gliding over and resting on my hip. I froze, the sheer heat and force of him sparking all kinds of primitive goose bumps over my body. "I was so absorbed in replying to an important email on my phone that I bumped into her, quite literally outside my local coffee shop. I was mortified, I spilled my coffee all over her. And like a fool I tried to help clean her coat with the only napkin I had. And despite my blubbering state she was so kind and well, it's embarrassing to admit but I knew even then, that she was the one. I'd never seen such a beautiful woman in my life. Although now I'd never be on my phone in front of her or she'd reprimand me," he chuckled while having a side dig at my expense. I offered a small laugh through gritted teeth. He obviously didn't like being ignored much in the cab. "And the rest is history, I've been lucky enough to be by her side ever since. I couldn't imagine a day without her."

There was an awkward silence. The story was so dramatic, dreamy and seemed utterly ridiculous. And yet, it worked.

"Wow, that's quite the story," Debra said, the veins in her neck presenting themselves as she inhaled deeply.

"Do you mind if I talk to my *boyfriend* for a moment?" I asked with a tight smile. I grabbed Damon and pulled him away. I marched him to the food buffet, ignoring his smirk.

"What are you doing?" I shot. He was unaffected by my tone.

"You wanted me to play the part of doting boyfriend didn't you? And she looks like she's about to burst a vein with pure jealousy right now. Are you not satisfied?" Damon rubbed his facial hair in contemplation.

I couldn't argue with him, but even I wasn't prepared for the avalanche of him turning on the act of Mr. Dreamy. "And we agreed, *no* pet names. You promised you'd be charming and cunning, and that you would fit in," I brooded.

"You're really not a romantic, are you?" Damon

collected a glass of champagne from a tray when a waiter walked past, then sipped on it casually as he scanned the room. I was taken back. How was I not romantic? No one met at a coffee shop like that! Well unless they were in some soap opera.

"I want a discount," I demanded, sure that no one could hear our conversation.

"You what?" he asked, raising an eyebrow and looking at me in puzzled amusement.

"I want a discount on your services. Right now, I'm not particularly happy. So, I want a discount."

Before Damon could say anything, the same cameraman from earlier interrupted us, asking for another photo. I smiled brightly, feeling triumphant after our small argument. I wrapped my hand around Damon's waist and placed my other on his chest before smiling brightly at the camera with a certain smugness. "Smile, dear."

Chapter 7

Damon

Her grip slipped away from me as soon as the photo was taken, leaving a lingering coldness behind. She smiled slyly as she took her next sip which encouraged me to take a mouthful of my own. Watching her and trying to figure out who she might be beneath the mask was mystifying as it was dangerous. A challenge of sorts.

It'd been a long time since I'd taken a playful liking toward any woman, especially a client of all people. I squared my shoulders, remembering the scorn of the last woman who I'd allowed to slip under my skin. I wouldn't let that happen again and that icy reminder fortified my resolve. This was after all, business.

Clover seemed unsettled by my lack of response

and relentless gaze. She grabbed my hand and dragged me toward the closest group of sponsors, immediately resuming her role. I filled in where I was needed or asked, but the woman was intelligent. She held her own in the room of powerful sponsors and reputable names, and I'd certainly caught the wandering eye from many toward her, even despite my presence beside her.

"I'll go get us another drink, Pookie Bear," I whispered into Clover's ear, tempted to nip at her just to see how she'd react. Would she become flushed or would she try and one-up me? Though from the way her body stiffened I knew I'd caught her attention either way. I threw her a wicked smile, pet names really did get under her skin. But if she had the courage to ask for a discount, I would make sure to have fun with it a little.

I headed to the bar and ordered us another drink, enjoying the moment of respite from the busy crowds. The suave music seemed to have tempted a few brave souls onto the dance floor.

"Is this your first type of event?" the woman who'd been flaunting the peacock mask asked me. The one and only Issobelle Sherain.

"I've been to one or two. I'm surprised you're not still surrounded." I gave her a polite smile. She was young and had become an overnight sensation. Amical but also only time would tell if she'd be able to keep up with her new lifestyle. I'd seen many drop into fame and riches and spoil it all, unable to handle its scrutinizing pressure.

"I made a getaway the moment I could," she laughed, flaring a pink fan despite the coolness of outside. "If I'm being honest, it's nice to be celebrated in such a way but, man, it's so hard talking to so many people about the same thing."

I laughed at that. "I know what you mean."

"You came in with Clover, didn't you?" she asked as she ordered her own cocktail. She leant back on her elbows studying the room just as I did. I watched Clover smiling and talking with the same group. Her gaze wandered over to us and then quickly diverted when she realized I was watching.

"I did." I smiled as the woman placed the red wine down and began pouring a glass of champagne.

"She's an incredible woman," Issobelle admired. "She set all of this up you know. It's a shame about her boss. Man, she's a bitch. Every good idea Clover had in our meetings, she'd cut it down. Even I can feel the tension." She drifted to meet my gaze and shrugged. "What? I'm sure you've met her as well. I wouldn't have signed exclusively to them if it wasn't such a good deal. But what's a girl to do? Someone has to pay for the rent in this overpriced city." Again, she shrugged, delightfully surprised when she was offered her cocktail at the same time, I was handed my champagne. "Cheers." She held out her glass, clinking it with mine, then sauntered off. Maybe Issobelle was levelheaded enough to keep it all together; it didn't seem like much bothered her.

I found Clover again, not surprised to find Gary monopolizing her. I wanted to intrude, not at all apologetic for making him uncomfortable. And there was the issue; unbeknownst to Clover, Gary fancied her, and his wife no doubt knew as well.

Chapter 8

Clover

"You look stunning tonight," Gary commented, not looking at me but at Damon who was standing on the other side of the room. His expression softened as he looked back at me with a smile that didn't reach his eyes. I felt slightly uncomfortable by his gaze. Usually when we spoke, others were around. Perhaps I felt unnerved by our earlier discussion. And oddly enough, I wished Damon were here with me now, to replace the thorny atmosphere of speaking with Gary alone.

I shook my head awkwardly with a light smile, trying to be polite while receiving the compliment. "Thank you."

Gary was always nice to me, despite his devilish wife. He continued, "I'm impressed with the organization of this as well. You've done a marvelous job as always."

"Thank you, but I had a few people help me on this one, so I can hardly take credit for it," I said, finding that I was craving Damon's company, already accustomed to his charisma that eased conversation around me.

Fingers brushed lightly along the back of my neck, sending a shiver through me. I turned to see Damon, who was smiling sweetly.

"Am I interrupting something?" Damon growled. His tone hitched my breath and forced Gary to step back as if *he* had been the one to walk into something.

"No, we were just talking." My tone was somewhat defensive, as if Damon had been accusing me of something. His dark-brown eyes steadily held mine and then met Gary's.

"I feel like dancing," he said, grabbing my hand. His surprisingly soft hand brushed over my fingertips.

"You what?" I asked. "Oh, honey, you know I don't dance." I smiled at him, but my eyes held a word of warning. My face conveyed the message, *I cannot dance.*

"Oh, but, my little angel puff, you know how I like to make you try. You're just so cute, even when you barter." Damon smiled wickedly.

I bit my tongue, understanding his message. This was his way of getting me back for my demand for a discount. He pulled on my hand and led me through the crowd to where a few people danced. I could tell from their stilted movements that they weren't nearly drunk enough yet to enjoy it.

"What are you playing at?" I asked as we stood in front of the band. He looked at me earnestly, placing his hand around my waist and holding my other hand lightly. He began to sway, and I tried to follow his lead. My awkwardness forced him to pull me in closer to control my hips, his chest brushing against mine. I forced out my forgotten breath so he wouldn't notice how his proximity affected me.

His hot breath rested on my ear for a moment before he spoke. "Checkmate," he taunted.

"Is this by chance a game to you?" I asked with a smile. My face had almost certainly gone red. My smile stretched wider as I looked over the clumps of people around us. "Do you patronize all your clients like this, or is there something you want to win?"

He suddenly pushed me away from him, and in perfect time with the music, he spun me under his arm before pulling me in fast and pressing my body against his in a fluid and controlled movement. I looked up at him, stunned, my breath once again lost. I couldn't look away from his teasing, molten brown eyes. I felt lost in them. I couldn't even remember what we were talking about.

"No, I don't usually do this to my other clients. But most don't challenge me the way you do. And I don't take losing lightly," he said with a cocky smile before slowly putting distance between us.

My breath came out staggered. I was embarrassed by my infatuation with him. It'd been so long since I was with a man that even his slightest touch lingered on my skin. His taunting words sparked an excitement in me I hadn't felt since... well, I couldn't even remember.

The tapping of a microphone rang out as Debra's voice echoed, "Testing." It brought reality back into the room. I stepped away, dropping Damon's hand. I smiled at the four band members, thanking them for their music as they fell into silence. Everyone began taking their seats at designated tables.

"We should sit down," I mouthed to Damon before collecting my glass of red wine on a nearby table. I knocked it back, hoping to relieve myself of the heat that built within my body. I sat down at our table, smiling at the few sponsors I was familiar with. Some were with partners, some with what may have been their own younger escorts.

As Damon took a seat beside me, I watched Drygo Biggs, who sat at a nearby table drinking brandy. He owned a large household items business that did well in the city, so big that he regularly sponsored us in return for discounted advertising in our online and printed magazines. He looked to be in his fifties. Beside him was a thin young blonde girl. She looked like she had only just graduated from university. She played with her silver hoop earrings and adjusted her strapless purple dress when she thought no one was looking. She would shoot Mr. Biggs an inviting smile when he looked at her hungrily. I questioned then whether she was an escort too.

Was it obvious that Damon was one? He did look out of my league. The idea of it clouded what I thought to be a victorious night. And as much fun as I had when my heart raced around Damon, I had to remind myself it was just business, and that it was a *lie*. I looked around at other couples, wondering whether anyone else had suspected him of being an escort.

Debra clapped as Issobelle Sherain took to the stage. Many speeches were to follow, and I sighed audibly. The fun was over for now. Damon furrowed his eyebrows and mouthed, "Are you all right?" I smiled reassuringly at him.

I had to call an escort. Did that make me pathetic? My mind drifted to my work situation as Issobelle droned on in the background, speaking of her countless inspirations. All the fun and excitement around Damon quickly vanished, as I found myself focusing on the workload I had to return to and the webpage I had no idea how to create. *Well, it was fun while it lasted,* I sighed to myself. Like Cinderella at her ball.

Everyone clapped loudly at the end of the speeches. The electric atmosphere had been dampened, and people began to take their leave, no doubt bound for the other glittering soirées of New York. Most lingered for a little longer. It was a prime opportunity to talk business and swap success stories. But I didn't have time for either. When I stood from my chair, straightening my dress, my eyes met with Debra's and she gave me a knowing smile. She knew what I had to look forward to at home. And it wasn't Damon.

"We should go now," I said to Damon, tightening

my grip on my clutch. Though I might've felt victorious for a moment, reality quickly sank back in. We said goodbye to a few of the sponsors nearby before walking out of the glass doors into the chilled night air. Damn it, I should've considered bringing a jacket.

We walked down a block so I could flag down a taxi and write out a check to Damon without the fear of someone seeing me do so. We stood in front of a little café which was still open. Inside were a few couples who chattered to one another over coffee and night owls working on their laptops. The city glowed with light and activity. We stepped into the opening of an alleyway and I pulled out my checkbook while Damon leaned against a wall. Shadows covered his face.

"How much?" I asked, already writing.

"Three hundred."

My mouth gaped open. "Wow, you charge that much?" Despite the shadows, I could see a playful smirk on his face. Before he could speak, I focused on my writing again. "Fine, but I'm clearly working in the wrong industry."

"You seem frazzled. Did you not have a good night?" Damon asked, leaning against the brick wall with his hands in his pockets.

"I did, it was fun, and thank you for helping me," I said, tugging off the check.

But this was just business, and the fun couldn't last forever. I gave Damon the check with an awkward smile. We stepped out onto the sidewalk, and I flagged down a taxi. It quickly pulled in for me.

"Thank you for tonight, really," I said again. He opened the door for me, watching me as I sank into the leather seat.

"It was lovely meeting you, Clover," he said with a genuine smile. It was surreal to believe this was his work and he did this for many women on a regular basis. Still, I couldn't pull my gaze away from his molten, dark-brown eyes. He was stunning, but even more so when the night's lights danced on his face, casting shadows under his masculine features—it only made me more curious as to what he looked like beneath the mask. I dropped my attention to his plump lips again, flustered by my own shamelessness.

"You too, Damon. Have a nice life," I said, regretting it instantly and closed the door behind me.

Who says have a nice life to an escort? I reprimanded myself.

I gave the cab driver my address, and as we pulled away, I dared to turn and have one more glimpse at my taunting, teasing, dazzling, cocky escort. He lifted his arm and stepped toward me. I too waved goodbye.

Chapter 9

Damon

H ad it been anyone else who'd done a runner on me, I might've let them escape. But not only did she have the hide to demand a discount, she also hadn't signed the cheque. It's not like I needed the money, but part of me felt like I wasn't entirely done teasing this woman. And I could just imagine her flustered expression when I outed her.

I tried calling her twice. No answer. Okay, little miss Cinderella... it's a shame I already have your address.

Standing at Clover's door, I realized I might've looked like a total stalker. I lifted my jacket sleeve to glance at my wrist watch. It was a little over eleven. Was I weirdo for following her to her address? No. What was owed was owed. And besides, she would've only arrived ten minutes before me. I rolled back my shoulders, unfamiliar with this lack of confidence. I cleared my throat and knocked on her door, imagining her flustered expression.

Clover opened the door skeptically, a fat orange cat bolting out the door. On reflex, I scooped the feline up before it made its dash past me. The little sucker had more weight to him than I'd expected.

Clover and I locked eyes, those soft brown eyes piercing me with surprise. She was so beautiful. Her makeup had been scrubbed off revealing unblemished tanned skin. She'd removed all the pins out of her hair, now thrown back into a wild, wavy pigtail. She looked far more comfortable in her gray sweatpants and loose orange shirt opposed to the dress she'd been wearing minutes ago.

"Damon?" she flustered. Ah yes, there was the risk that without my mask she might recognize who I was.

"I believe this is yours," I said, handing over the orange cat who'd already bit at my hand to let him down.

She collected him unnerved. "Sorry, he always tries to run for the door. I'm... What are you doing here?" A release of tension seemed to ripple through me; she obviously didn't recognize me.

"You didn't sign the check," I said with a smug smile.

It seemed to dawn on her then. "Oh my gosh. I thought you were waving goodbye to me, I didn't realize you were flagging me down. Come in, I'm so sorry."

Despite the exterior of the building and hallway, the inside was nicely renovated and refurbished. Reaching the kitchen, she seemed in a fluster as she searched through her drawers for a pen. Despite the exterior of the building and hallway, the inside was nicely renovated and refurbished. As nice as it was... it also felt empty with a few essentials. The liveliest thing in here was the fat cat now rubbing against my leg. I bent over to scratch behind his ear.

By the time Clover had turned around he'd decidedly swatted my hand away. Temperamental little thing. "Sorry, he does that." She tried to usher him away as she straightened her shirt. "Pudding, go eat your food."

"Pudding?" My smile widened. "You called your cat Pudding but don't like pet names?" I held tongue in cheek, trying not to laugh.

With a hand on her hip she seemed affronted.

"It's a long story. And besides, he has no say in what he's called. I do."

"I don't know maybe that's why he's biting everyone..." I teased.

"I'll have you know, he was very fond of the name. And besides it was kinder than saying pudgy. He doesn't much like that word. Do you have the check?"

I pulled out my wallet and handed it to her as I looked around the humble apartment. The smell of hazelnut coffee drew my attention to the open laptop on her desk. I put my wallet on the fish tank, curious by her work.

"What's this?" I asked while idly rubbing over my hand that Pudding had sunk his little fangs into. The open tab of many boldly stated: *How to Insert a Website Page for Dummies*.

She seemed embarrassed. "Um... Debra, wants me to add a website page to our website by midnight, but I have no idea how," she admitted, offering me back the signed check. Midnight? I checked my watch again. If she didn't know how to build one now she'd never reach that time, even an expert in the field would struggle with that timeframe.

"May I?" I asked, indicating the chair and laptop.

"Do you usually barge into your clients' homes

72

and make yourself comfortable?" she joked, bestowing me with a lazy smile and a nod.

"Only the ones who do a runner on me." I grinned, assessing the open screens. She blushed red, readjusting her shirt.

"I don't have much time left though so I really need to finish it."

I briefly read over the mission statement. It was an easy enough program I could work around. "I can do this for you now if you'd like?"

"What?" I twisted in her chair lazily to face her.

"I can do this for you. I have a background in this kind of stuff. You won't make that deadline without my help."

I could tell she was flushed with my honest remark and if looks could kill I almost expected her to throw me out into the hallway and slam the door in my face. She was sensitive about her ability to perform. I wasn't surprised.

"And what else would that cost me?" she asked, crossing her arms.

A lazy smile spread across my face. *Interesting*. "How about another hazelnut coffee and a thank you."

She pondered over it for a moment, suspicious. "How about I start that coffee then," she smiled tightly. The tension in her seemed to drop. "And thank you. To be honest I was at my wit's end with it already."

She walked into the kitchen as I continued searching over the design, asking her questions about the vision she had. After making the coffee, she pulled a dining chair beside me, comfortable with her coffee in hand as she kindly criticized my progress. Despite not being able to execute it herself, she knew exactly what she wanted and where.

"So then you drag this here," she said, immersed in my work as she leaned over and pointed to the screen. The scent of her lingering perfume hit me all at once. I straightened due to her proximity, enticing an entirely different part of me that responded to her closeness. "And it'll stay like that?" she asked, facing me. As if suddenly aware of our close proximity, she immediately sat back in her chair, that light flush streaking her cheeks.

"Yes," I said glancing over at the fish tank as a distraction. Why was this woman getting under my skin? I was around beautiful women all the time so why was I so fascinated by her? What made her so special? But the last time I thought someone was special it completely destroyed me.

I ignored the reminder and continued busily

typing in codes. I was distracted by her taking peeks at my side profile. "What is it?" I asked. She sat back in her chair cradling Pudding in her arms and scratching his belly.

"I'm just curious, how does an escort acquire the skills to do this?" I briefly rubbed at my eyes, my contacts starting to irritate after wearing them all day.

"I'm not a full-time escort, you know," I said, giving her a brief glance. It was refreshing for once, someone not knowing who I actually was.

She nibbled at her bottom lip as if wanting to ask more but then a small smile appeared instead. I found my gaze lingering on her lips for far too long.

"What are you smiling at?" I asked, unable to hide my own curious smile, as if it were contagious.

"Nothing," she replied and collected our empty mugs. "Would you like another coffee, or I even have juice and water?"

"I'll just have some water if I can, I'm almost done here anyway." Saving the new design with six minutes to spare before midnight, I then clicked on another open document. Briefly reading over the article, I was touched by its beautiful flow. "Did you write this?" I asked, looking over my shoulder.

"Didn't your mother ever lecture it's bad to

snoop?" she called out as she walked over with the glasses of water.

"I would hardly consider an already open file that's meant for the webpage as snooping," I argued. Her eyes seemed to twinkle with mischief as she offered me the water.

"I did, although Debra won't be happy with it. It isn't the original piece. *That* was somehow magically lost," she said sarcastically.

I wanted to ask her why she put up with a belittling boss, but much like I appreciated her not inquiring further into my personal life, I respected her in the same light. "It's good. Your voice really shines through," I complimented before adding the article as the last missing piece.

"Thank you," she said sincerely, grabbing my attention again. There was something raw in her response. "It's silly, but my father used to read all my pieces in our local newspaper at Ithaca, even the unpublished ones that I found far more interesting to write. No one has read any of my work for a while now. It feel's almost scary to share it again," she seemed to laugh to herself.

"You say that as if he isn't around anymore?" I deliberated cautiously.

"He's not. A heart attack took him from us. But I

still remember how he used to criticize and compliment my work like a compliment sandwich," she sadly laughed to herself. My body ran cold. I knew all too well what it was like to lose a parent, it'd destroyed my father and left our family business in shambles.

"I'm sorry for your loss." And although I could relate to her pain, I withdrew from vocalizing it.

"Thank you. And it was nice to think about it, so thank you. Are you a writer?"

"Are you trying to snoop about my personal life, Angel Puff?"

She scoffed at the pet name. I chuckled as I finalized the webpage. "That's all set up now and live."

I stretched out my back, satisfied by my work. "Well, now you can say we're even for that discount you were after." I took a mouthful of the water and shrugged my coat back on.

"Wait," she said seriously. "You didn't give me a discount in the first place?" She was smiling, her loose shirt hanging over her shoulder as she closed her laptop. "Thank you, for all of this. You've not only saved me my job, but I had a really nice night as well."

I found myself staring blankly at her, restraining my male urges to pull her closer. There was something enticing about her sincerity. Maybe it'd been too long since I bedded a woman. Alex might've been right, and now I was even considering a client of all people. I rounded my shoulders again, straightening my jacket. "That's my job," I said, making a point to pocket the check. "Once again, I'm glad you're happy with my services, and if you need to be escorted again, you have my card."

Clover seemed unsettled and it was no doubt because of my shift in demeanor. We'd been having fun, yes. But this was make-believe and our roles for tonight had come to a halt.

"Of course, thank you for everything. I hope it'll get Debra off my back for a little while yet." She politely smiled.

"Yea, well I think we put her off a little, and you definitely beat her at her own game tonight," I said, shuffling closer to the door. "I hope you have a good night."

"You too," she said after me as I walked out into the hallway. I felt like I needed out for fresh air ASAP before I did something I'd regret and act on impulse alone. Something about that woman crawled under my skin... and all in the right ways. I loosened my tie, feeling hot under the pressure. Tonight, *I was an escort.*

Chapter 10

Damon

I could count the amount of times I'd misplaced something in my life on one hand. And yet somehow, I'd misplaced my wallet and the last place I remembered putting it down was on the fish tank at Clover's apartment. The wallet didn't matter. What was even more alarming was my sudden need to leave her apartment, unsure of my intense urges towards her. And now I find myself in a unique situation.

"Look at you all fresh Monday morning," Alex commented as he walked into the boxing ring at our gym. I was already pouring sweat from my five-mile run. Granted, I was here earlier than normal, but I wasn't able to sleep the night before. I felt dishevelled in my state, shirt thrown to the side as I fixed my gloves on, panting like a madman. I felt like I had so much excess energy to burn.

"I wish I could say the same for you, late night again?"

He shrugged as he began stretching on the outside mats. This early in the morning, only a few others had started filtering into the gym. In spite of having my own home gym, Alex introduced me to boxing and I had to admit that over the last twelve months it has helped. And so, no matter how hung over he might've been- he always made sure to show up as well. And I was certain that was more for my sake than his.

"I sent you a text message to join me. It was a pretty incredible night." He sparkled with mischief.

"And who was she this time?" I asked with very little interest in his answer. She was just another number to Alex.

He seemed wounded. "You think so little of me?" But even he couldn't hold in the smile. Alex liked the chase and he never slept with a woman twice. Those were his "rules." It didn't make him a bad guy, but that was the problem, women became attached quickly because he was a nice guy. Successful too.

"I'm just saying I think it'd be good if you got out once and a while."

I fell silent, my thoughts racing back to Clover and the very exceptional time out I had.

"Look, I know with everything that happened with Michael and Annabelle really scorned you but I think—"

I cut him off. "I don't want to talk about it."

"Everyone's worried about you. You've laid low for long enough now and you were never in the wrong. You need to stop punishing yourself over this."

I exhaled, my patience wearing thin. Best friend or not, I wasn't ready for another pep talk. From him or my sister.

"You know you can still trust me right," he said wearily. "I'd never do what Michael did to you."

I bit back my next words. There was no reason to lash out at Alex out of anger because of what Michael did. But I wasn't a child. I didn't need people "looking after me." Of course, I knew he wouldn't do that to me. Did he think I was punishing him because of it?

"I know and I do." Tension seemed to ripple out of me. Alex seemed relieved as he hoisted himself up and strapped the boxing pads onto his hand, clapping them together, ready for the sparring match.

"How about this weekend, you and me hit the town, just like old times," he encouraged.

I punched a few sets, the focused rhythm of my own breath seeming to jitter away some of that excess buzzing energy at the mention of Michael's and Annabelle's names.

"I'm not a complete shut in, you know," I said on the next hit.

Alex's eyebrow arched. "Oh? Does this mean someone's been getting jiggy?" he said with a suave smile but never taking his eye off the set.

I hit again, the slap of fist to mat encouraging me to go harder and faster. Dust fragmented around us. The outside glass panels still only mirroring the outside city lights. It'd be another hour until the sun would come up.

"I'm not getting jiggy with anyone," I said through a coarse breath.

"So there is someone?" he said, delightfully surprised. I exhaustedly swung and bounced back. His legs danced rapidly as he swung into uppercuts on his own, as if spurring me on. "That's my boy!"

I wiped at the sweat on my brow, trying not to childishly smile at his theatrics. It'd only encourage him more.

"I told you there's no one."

"You might fool someone else Damon Brogardt but I've known you for long enough, to know when you're keeping a dirty little secret. I'll wait. We still have time for a coffee and bagel so you can tell me all about it."

Shaking my head, I stepped back into rhythm. For the most part he did know everything about me, except of course the escorting business I created on the side two years ago. And I had no intention of telling him about Clover. That seemed inconceivable. My stomach dropped at the thought of her going through my wallet, because then she would discover who I was. A dread washed over me at how she might use it against me or to her own gain. I'd learnt that lesson the hard way.

Chapter 11

Clover

Curiosity was an interesting thing, and yet my morals punished me before I even dared to snoop through Damon's wallet. But oh, how I wanted to. I'd sent him a text to let him know he'd left it behind, which he hadn't yet replied to. It seemed like we were playing a game of cat and mouse. I tried to reason with myself, especially the part that seemed exhilarated to see him again. I was embarrassed by my own fantasy. I was still a woman at heart, but a part of me had forgotten—or more specifically neglected—that for a long time.

I joined the hordes of other *Candice* employees in the reception area Monday morning. With coffee in hand, I straightened the purple ruffled blouse I was wearing and my gray pencil skirt. Our department floor was barren at 7:00 a.m. The only other person enthused enough to dive into their work so early in the morning was Debra, who was scraping through paperwork. I begrudgingly admired her work ethic through the ceiling-high glass walls. The sun began to glow orange behind her as it rose above the awakening city. *Another early morning we get to spend together*, I grimaced sarcastically to myself.

I stopped at Cassidy's desk to admire the purple flowers that sat on her round, white marbled reception desk, noticing the card that read: From Debra and Gary. I placed the small bag of gold hoop earrings beside the flowers. I hoped she'd like them, especially considering she told me abruptly these were what she wanted for her birthday as she pointed to their advertisement in a magazine. I left my own small note beside the gift, keeping it short and sweet with a "Happy Birthday, Beautiful. Clover." She'd definitely have a mountain of presents by the end of the day, everyone loved Cassidy. She had the lighthearted summery nature where it seemed like nothing could go wrong. People gravitated to that naturally.

I could sense Debra scowling at me as I set up my desk. *If she hated me that much, why didn't she just fire me?* My temperament was much more sensitive today than usual, and I swallowed my irritation. All I could think of was the impression that Damon had—that I was unhappy at work. I slumped into my chair and stared at the photo of Megan and me on my desk. I'd never taken the time to think of it before, so why now?

The glass door between Debra's office and my own silently opened as she entered without invitation. She positioned herself on the corner of my desk, crossing her legs intimidatingly. She was silent for a moment—all part of the torture. "The article posted wasn't the one I sent you; did you take it upon yourself to write your own story?"

I gritted my teeth, not wanting to say the first thought that came to mind, which was an accusation. I was nearly certain it was her that hadn't transferred the correct details over.

"When I opened the files, it wasn't there, so I improvised," I retorted sharply.

"Clover, do you think this magazine runs on improvised decisions? You're very lucky I'm not issuing you with a written warning for such behavior. It'll still have to be changed today, so really you have created more work for everyone else."

"I understand," I said through gritted teeth. "Anything else?"

"Yes, Marcial has handed in his resignation. He's supposed to give two weeks' notice, but there are some outside circumstances to consider. So, I'd like it if you could organize a small party of sorts for him on Friday the end of *this* week to say goodbye," she said casually, taking another sip of her coffee and crossing her legs again.

"You want it organized for Friday?"

"Yes, oh, feel free to invite your dazzling boyfriend. You two left so quickly Saturday night I never got to say goodbye. I still can't believe that *you* obtained such a fine specimen," she said, brushing through her fringe and neatening her bun. "I still can't believe it."

"I'm sorry but he won't be able to make it. He has a busy work schedule," I quipped. It only worsened the situation because she thrived off my unclipped replies. She was waiting to find anything to taunt me over.

"Well then, perhaps he's not as dedicated to you as you had us believe. But don't be alarmed, we all have short, fun relationships to get us by here and there. Not everyone is meant for a loyal, long-term relationship," Debra said indignantly.

Before I could reply, she sauntered out of the room and sharply shut the door between our offices tightly behind her. I bit my lip, holding back the bitter taste her conversation left in my mouth. Why did I stand for this? I felt like I was ready to scream.

My boyfriend, huh? I thought of Damon, agitated with myself for thinking of him straight away. Now what was I to do? I couldn't call him and ask him to attend this party. It was a stupid game to get involved with in the first place. Why had I agreed to her webbed games? I felt no more victorious today than I did when I silently accepted her challenge last Friday.

I started scrolling through my contacts to find Lismoore's Catering. They were used to catering for us at short notice, thanks to Debra. While emailing them, my mind constantly raced over Damon's brown, molten eyes, his husky voice, that taunting smile, and how he rubbed his facial hair. My lie had cast a ripple effect. He was in the back of my mind, on repeat, torturing me in a heated fluster. What would I say in the coming weeks... "We broke up"? Wouldn't that only give Debra more satisfaction? I hadn't thought through the long-term repercussions of this lie.

I looked at my phone hopelessly, for some reason expecting a message or a missed call. I was hoping to hear from Damon, I realized. *It's because I have his wallet,* I convinced myself. I rolled my eyes at my infatuation. Was it because he was someone new? Someone I could laugh with? I scratched at my hair in confused agitation. Why was Damon all I was thinking of? I felt like I was losing my mind.

Colleagues began trailing in, and eventually the lady of the day, Cassidy, sounded her arrival with a squeal of delight. I clicked out of my screen and walked out to her desk, thankful I could focus on someone else.

"Happy birthday!" She tucked her curly blonde hair behind her ears, smiling as she opened the jewelry box.

"Thank you! I love them." She beamed, exchanging the earrings she wore for the hoops. "How did you know?" she asked, feigning surprise. She looked in her small compartment mirror with admiration. She did love them.

"So, how was Saturday night? I already snuck in a peek of him by the photos Liam printed. He looked so hot! And oh my gosh, the mystery of what his face might look like beneath. Tell me everything!"

Cassidy didn't delay in asking the questions, and I should've known better than to think I'd get away with *not* talking about Damon. "I don't really want to get into it too much," I said sheepishly. I felt like it was my little secret and I was nervous I'd say too much or blubber on. I'd sound like I was utterly infatuated with him.

"Um I'm sorry but there's an unspoken rule that if you hire an escort, you *must* tell your girlfriends everything!"

"It was interesting," I said coyly, trying to keep the blush from streaking my cheeks. Except I *had* seen his face because we'd spent more hours at my place. "I had a really nice night." I drifted into silence as one of the journalists exited the elevator and headed to the journo's room.

"So did you get lucky?" she asked with a sly smile before poking out her tongue.

"Of course not!"

Cassidy's jaw dropped surprised by my outright rejection. I instantly regretted how loudly I'd said it and searched the nearby offices to make sure no one was looking my way.

"He's an escort, not a prostitute."

"What a shame. You guys looked cute in the photo," she said while straightening her pink, mid-length dress and then jumping onto her bench casually to sit, childishly swinging her legs back and forth.

"Well, I don't know what to do now, because

Debra expects him to come to Marcial's going-away party, which obviously isn't going to happen, but I feel like I perhaps shouldn't have played into her game."

"Marcial's leaving?"

"Yea, I only found out this morning as well. Debra's making me organize a party for him. But she expects me to bring Damon along. And I don't know what to do. I thought it would be fun Saturday night —and it was—but it was a lie, all the same."

"So invite him, hire him out again?" Cassidy simply said, looking at the few gifts piled on her desk. She ripped a purple ribbon from a silver-wrapped gift.

"It's not that simple," I hesitantly said. Her eyebrows rose, and she leaned forward with anticipation.

"What happened?" she asked, utterly immersed.

"It was nothing, it's just... I don't know. He came back to my apartment after the campaign and helped me with that website page I had to organize. And it was nice, like, really nice. And I don't know, we were talking, and then we were kind of staring at one another with an awkward tension. And then he couldn't have run any faster out my door," I babbled, embarrassed by what had happened.

"You like him!" she exclaimed, quieting her next words as a few people in the office turned to stare at us. "You like your escort, well... all the more reason to invite him. Who knows, it might be a secret forbidden love. Oh my, how dare the escort fall in love with his client. Just like in a movie."

"Shut up." I pushed her lightly, amused by her theatrics. She laughed to herself before pushing back her blonde curls again. I continued in a whisper, "He actually left his wallet at my house... but he hasn't replied to my message."

"Maybe he left it there on purpose." Cassidy winked with a wicked smile.

Although I wished that were the case, I highly doubted it.

"I think you should hire him again," she continued.

Debra cleared her throat, grabbing our attention. "Clover, I don't pay you to stand around and make jokes. I've just sent through some templates I need you to look over," she said sternly before walking toward the journo's room.

Cassidy sighed, her excitement deflated. "She really doesn't like you."

"More than ever today, for some reason," I tried to joke.

When I sat down at my desk, I opened a new email from Liam. It'd been sent to all staff members based on our campaign success Saturday night. There were numerous photos of Issobelle Sherain and a lot of sponsors who looked well-fed and merry. My speedy mouse-clicking stopped when I came across one picture. It was one of Damon and me after I'd just demanded a discount from him. I compared the photo to the one on my desk where I was with Megan. It was the same smile— one when I was genuinely enjoying myself.

I exited out of the email and checked my phone again. Still no reply. *Because it was only business,* I reminded myself. It was nothing more and nothing less. So why was my heart beating erratically and I felt on edge, waiting for his reply?

Chapter 12

Damon

I t wasn't until midday that I had time to check the cell hidden in the top drawer of my desk. The morning had been full of meetings and projections of our next financial year. Clover sent me a message advising I'd left my wallet at hers. I didn't need it. Like most things, it was dispensable, and yet I wanted to make the effort collect it. Clover was so outside of my usual circle, so different to the social expectation and demands of my world. And part of me wanted to step out of that again, like spending time with her was an excuse to explore something new. And I had no idea what to make of it.

A light knock on my door stole away my attention from my computer. Instead of Alex letting himself in, it was Michelle. Her dark-brown hair pinned back tightly.

"Hello, little brother," she teased while keeping her eye out in the main hallway. "Alex seems wounded that I asked for your time privately. He's sulking out there and waiting for his turn."

"Does he have a coffee in his hand?" I asked.

She stepped back to do a double take. "Yes."

"Then I'm sad too."

"He seems more uncomfortable by Sotiny sitting beside him than me kicking him out." Her curious watchful gaze lingered for a moment longer until finally she closed the door. "I'm telling you, there's tension between those two. They have history."

"I don't ask much about Alex's conquests."

"Or maybe not conquests, and that's the problem," she said, wickedly delighted in the prospect. Very few saw this side of my sister. They only saw their CEO. Alex was one of few who'd seen Michelle outside of work mode, and even then she ran a tight ship.

"I'm sure you didn't visit me to talk about your personal assistant and our head of marketing's lack of rendezvous?"

"Well, I have to live vicariously through the young people." It went without saying that Alex was only a few years younger than her. "Married life can seem so routine," she paraded. I rolled my eyes. Greg was the love of her life, and sometimes, the anchor to her demanding flair.

She sat across from me, taking the leather chair and looking around the room as if newly discovered. Well, it had been some time since she was last in here. I had the shades down, blocking out the light and noise from the outside world. "Your hair's longer," she remarked.

"I'm having it cut Thursday," I commented as I leaned back into my chair.

"Don't do that power play thing with me," she jabbed as she crossed one leg over the other, the perfect cut of intimidation. It would appear we were at a standoff yet again.

"Are we going to have another battle of wits, sister?" I asked, exhausted. I hadn't met anyone as headstrong as my sister. And I loved her dearly. I respected her for her work ethic and being the heart of this company. But she could also be extremely annoying. She didn't leave much room for error, let alone leniency. And that included her family.

"I don't want to fight you," she simply said.

"Then why do you say that with a battle-ready tone?"

"Don't patronize me. Have you spoken to Dad recently?" We stared at one another, mirroring the usual standoff we'd done ever since we were children.

"No, I've been busy."

"You know he has concerns. We all do," she embellished.

"I told you, you don't need to check up on me. *Their* breaking up hasn't spiraled me. I've laid low. I've continued working and—"

"It's not about work, Damon, and you know it. Yes, you've taken a step back from the social circles. No, I haven't seen you splattered on a magazine or dodgy online article for months. But that was never my concern. Our reputation as a family and company was always going to uphold. What I'm worried about is how you're doing. You've been gloomy ever since that article came out about Michael and Annabelle breaking up." My entire body went rigid at the mere mention of her. Where Alex was tactful to restrain himself, my sister didn't give a flying damn. "I'm worried that you'll act hastily. Try and take her back."

My teeth ground. I couldn't think of anything worse or more diabolical. Did they really think I was that desperate and lonely? "It's been two years. And what would I care, the child's not mine, remember?" I begrudgingly added. I wasn't bound to Annabelle in any way other than history. And it took all my strength not to openly seethe my hatred.

Her shoulders sagged. "No, it's not but it's just a reminder of how quickly time has already slipped by. Don't you want to move on? I'm just scared there's some part of her that still has hold over you."

"She humiliated me," I gritted out, restraining myself from opening that spiteful hurt on my sister. But I was so over people tiptoeing around me at the mention of their names or gossip from mutual friends. I wanted the past to remain where it should be. Behind me. "She never owned me as all of you so insistently seem to bring up."

"No, she hurt you, brother," Michelle corrected. "If you say it's fine and you're not moping about or burying your head in the sand, then fine. But you forget I was there too, with you. I know how much you loved her. I just want to make sure you're moving on and happy. I don't want you to be only consumed by work. That's never helped anyone," she said softly.

"Projecting are we?" I said scornfully.

Her lips went thin and the vulnerability of being my sister was barricaded by the CEO again. "Yes, which is why I'm telling you, only you will hurt from this. Call Dad sometime, he misses you. And for goodness' sake open up those blinds. You look like a depressed teenager," she chided as she stood up and waltzed out.

Begrudgingly, I did as she said, knowing that she was right. More than anything right now, I needed some fresh air because old wounds were resurfacing. Things I'd buried deep a long time ago, and I had no interest in revisiting the ghosts of the past.

Chapter 13

Clover

What Cassidy wanted, she got. And birthday drinks at one of the local sports bars on the corner to celebrate her twenty-sixth birthday was exactly what she wanted. A group of us gathered after work, helping with the excessive bags of presents she'd hauled throughout the day.

"First round of shots are on Luis," Cassidy clapped as he struggled to help carry her bags.

"You wish," he replied as we swarmed into the main reception on the first level, bumping into Issobelle Sherain. Gossip had spread through the office that she'd had issues with her first feature model during their shoot today. And by taking in her tired expression, I believed it.

"Hey, Issobelle," Cassidy called out and waved, the big helium balloon bouncing around her wrist. As usual, Issobelle was stylishly dressed in an edgy way, but looked depleted after the day's work. "Do you want to come out for some drinks? We're just celebrating the fabulous me."

So far, there were only six of us, and I hadn't actually seen Cassidy talk with Issobelle, but like always her personality drew everyone in like a moth to flame. When it came to parties, Cassidy lived by the philosophy "The more the better."

Issobelle surveyed our group, her gaze landing on me. Perhaps I was the only one she was familiar with so far and with a slight shrug she said, "Sure why not, I had a shitty model today so I might as well drink to something."

Luis nervously laughed and collectively we were at a loss as to what to say. Her featured model was a famous local chef, and she so casually flipped him off without a care in the world. And yet I admired her directness. We left the *Candice* building, a weight immediately rippling off me.

"Oh wow, it *is* my birthday," Cassidy giggled as her gaze landed on the man waiting in front of the *Candice Magazine* building. In a salmon shirt and a black buttoned jacket, he leaned against a chic black car. My jaw dropped. Even the dark shades couldn't entirely conceal his identity. It was like his mask all over again except I'd remember that cocky lazy stance anywhere.

"Damon?" I stumbled on my next step. "What are you doing here?"

"*The* Damon?" Cassidy bounced in excitement as she stepped forward to inspect him closer.

"We'll be two seconds." I hurriedly filled the space between us, conscious of everyone's nosy gaze.

"I'm Cassidy," she said enthusiastically and held out her hand. She titled her head to the side. "Have I seen you somewhere before?"

With a suave smile he shook her hand delicately. "Possibly, Manhattan isn't as big as some suggest."

She beamed another smile. "He definitely was money well spent, wasn't he?"

"Cassidy!" I reprimanded her. Damon's eyebrows shot up and she chuckled, delighted by both of our reactions.

"I'm just teasing. Well since you seem to have a date, I'll be on my merry way, but you both owe me a drink," she pointed to both of us and then sauntered away. End of discussion.

"Wait!"

Cassidy ignored me, wrapping her arms around

Luis and Issobelle. She tugged them away as their prying eyes ogled over Damon and me, a flutter of questions unsaid.

"Come on, guys, today's about me, remember," Cassidy taunted, effortlessly refocusing the group back onto her. And as easily as that, I was ditched. I was almost affronted. Even when I didn't go out with them often, I was so easily dispensable.

"What are you laughing about?" I asked Damon inquisitively, as he chuckled to himself.

His hands were tucked into the pockets of his pants. "Cassidy seems nice, and... determined. What did you tell her about my services?" Although he was still smiling, I could hear a hint of curiosity in his tone.

I cleared my throat, adjusting my scarf slightly. "Cassidy was the one who gave me your card so of course she had a lot of questions after our night. Not much more to tell. Anyway, what are you doing here?"

"You have my wallet, remember?"

"Well yea, but you never replied to my text. And I don't have it on me, it's back at my apartment."

"I thought I'd replied..." He seemed perplexed. Whatever Mr. Escort was during the day, he didn't seem to be one to forget things.

"Damon, what a pleasant surprise to see you, again," Debra called out as she sauntered from the building. Part of me wanted to step in front of Damon, irritated by her ogling gaze. A desire to claim him in front of her, just to irk her, but then remembered the reason why I was in this situation in the first place. This was all fake. And Damon was certainly not my anything.

"Ah, Debra, I hope you're keeping warm during the weather we've been having."

"I'm born and raised in Manhattan, there's nothing this weather could do that would surprise me." She leered over me as if I was imposing on their private conversation. "Clover was telling me you were too busy to attend our little get together Friday night, that seems like a shame to me."

"Get together?" he queried.

"Oh she hasn't told you yet. Well, I hope that's the only secret between you two," she joked with spiteful glee in her eye. "I hope to see you then."

The woman had a natural talent for being condescending and when she did it in front of Damon, it both embarrassed and infuriated me. I unfurled my fingers from my tight grasp.

"Is she like this toward you every day?" he politely asked.

"She's a bit easier to manage on the days I slip valium into her coffee." He didn't at all understand my dry sarcasm. "I'm kidding."

I nervously laughed it off, not wanting to honestly answer him. Did he pity me? That was more mortifying. "We can catch a cab back to mine so you can pick up your wallet, it's not a problem. Now that my loyal colleagues have ditched me it would appear I'm free."

"Give me one second," Damon said before leaning in to whisper to the driver who'd brought him here.

"Or we can go in your lift, I don't mind," I suggested. But just as quickly the car drove off into the bustling traffic. "Don't dare tell me you have your own chaperone," I jested.

"I'm a man of great mystery," he teased as he flagged down another yellow cab. I wasn't entirely sure if he was joking, but the mystery held truth. "Ladies first."

It still seemed strange to me. Spending time with this man who I knew nothing about, especially considering the circumstances that brought us together. I shuffled into the back of the cab, offering the driver my address.

I side-eyed Damon again. His cologne seemed to

envelope me making the distance feel nonexistent between us. I was acutely aware of how closely our hands rested next to one another and mortified by how much it affected me.

"What is it?" he asked. His rough voice sent a tingle through my body. *Calm down Clover, you're not a raging teenager. This is a business transaction.*

"I was just thinking how different you look without your mask and suit," I flushed quickly, immediately regretting why I'd even mention his appearance.

"When I arrived at your apartment last night, you were wearing sweatpants," he reminded me with his eyebrows raised playfully.

"Touché'."

"So, what are you going to do about your ingenious Fake Boyfriend plan," he teased as he casually leaned against the door and landed that curious unrelenting gaze on me. There was an intensity to him that I didn't notice through the mask. It was unnerving only because I was so conscious of his every little move.

Did I seem pathetic to him, needing to pretend that someone would actually be willing to date me just to "one-up" my boss? Debra would only ask more questions about him and the reality was, it was only circumstantial that he was even with me now. "Well, I guess I'm going to have to be honest."

"I still don't understand why you just don't move on. If your boss makes your life a living hell, why don't you find another job or send through some online submissions and freelance projects?" he asked sympathetically.

I held in my sigh. I felt vulnerable around him and talking about my work. It made me feel almost like I'd failed to a degree. But he wouldn't understand that, how could he, we'd only just met. "It's a competitive market. Even in my role now I know should be grateful. I *am* grateful and I really need to make this work. And besides why are you asking me these questions when you won't tell me anything about yourself?"

"Touché'," he added. And it felt like a slap in the face. I don't know why I'd expected anything further. He was after all an escort, not my friend, not even my acquaintance. Just a stranger I'd hired for a night.

The taxi crawled to a stop. "It looks like there's an accident ahead," he said, looking through the mirror. "We might be here for a while."

"It's only three blocks away, we could always walk," I suggested.

Damon was staring outside the window, his eyes wide in shock.

"Damon?" I asked slowly, unsure why it suddenly looked like he'd seen a ghost.

"Can we get out here?" he asked.

"Well yea that's what I was just suggesting."

He handed the cab driver cash with a generous tip. "Thank you." He rounded the cab before I could even open the door for myself. He led me through the traffic that beeped and honked with no progress being made. I briefly peered over at the scene of the incident. From where I could see, everyone looked okay. A little shaken but okay.

"They seem okay," Damon reassured. "Do you mind if we stop by for a coffee here?"

Was this the place he'd been looking at through the window? He seemed to have returned to his usual self but now there was something else there. Something innocent, maybe even childlike. I couldn't entirely tell because of the dark shade of his glasses but his demeanor had changed slightly.

"Sure." I couldn't read Damon like most people. I had no idea what was going through his mind. Was this a novelty for him? Was I just entertainment? Or would someone, outside of this situation looking in, consider it a date?

He admired the small cafe bookstore, taking it in with something more, familiarity perhaps. I'd driven past it every day but never considered stopping. The storefront held a rustic charm of sorts. Despite the chill, some customers still sat outside on the white slick chairs. Little potted purple plants grew under the large bay windows.

He held the door open for me, gesturing for me to enter first. The mixture of old books and roasted coffee tantalized my senses. It was a familiar and relaxing smell. I'd always loved to read but couldn't remember the last time I'd had a chance to pick up a book for leisure.

Slim white bookshelves wrapped around the room, closing in the small coffee counter on my left. A small wooden spiral staircase led to another level with more bookshelves. On the right were purple leather booths and white marble tables each ornamented with a potted fake plant.

It was shameful that this was so close to my apartment, yet I'd never ventured in. Damon walked over to the young barista, who was smiling at us welcomingly.

"Two hazelnut lattes, please?" he asked politely, looking at me for reassurance. I nodded approvingly, surprised that he'd remembered my favorite coffee.

"Thank you."

While we waited for our coffee, I skimmed over the bookshelves in front of the booth area. I found myself captivated by the travel section, gliding my fingers along the spines and landing on one about Japan.

"Any books capture your attention?" Damon asked. I found it bizarre that he was still wearing his glasses, even indoors. Sometimes practicality didn't always reach the lines of a fashionable piece. He was already holding a brown paper bag filled with books after his own brief exploration.

"You read?" I asked, pointing at the bag, curious as to what kind of books they might be.

"Of course I read." He charmed a crooked smile. "I'm starting to think you've judged me harshly."

"No," I said ambiguously. "But in all honesty, I still don't know what I think of you." I narrowed my gaze on him in mock suspicion.

"Only good things, I'd hope." He gestured we take our conversation toward one of the booths. "Should we sit?"

We took a booth near the window. There was a couple in the corner giggling to one another, and a student behind us studying with headphones while slurping on his coffee.

"I read some of your pieces," Damon admitted. "Online... from the Ithaca newspaper."

"You've been checking up on me?" I asked in surprise. My heart lightly fluttered, embarrassed by the way I so obviously reacted to him. *Why would he be interested in me?*

"Out of intrigue, maybe. My favorite piece was probably about the neighborhood cat and dog that regularly got into a fight. I can't believe you managed to write a whole article on that with feverish passion." He laughed.

I began laughing, playing with my earring as nostalgia hit me. "Hey, don't judge it, if you were there, you would know. It was hilarious, you should've seen their respective owners trying to split them up and chase them home." My smile brightened, and I laughed even harder at the memory. I still can't believe they printed that piece. "It was my greatest piece," I teased.

"I have no doubt," he said, practically drinking in my laughter. It felt contagious. With a delicate smile he asked, "So if you had all that there, why did you come to Manhattan to be a personal assistant?"

I considered him for a moment. He seemed to ask a lot of questions for someone who wasn't willing to divulge any personal information about himself.

"I'll make a deal with you, mysterious Damon. If I answer your questions you have to give me something genuine about yourself in return. That's how this works."

"Is it just?" He smiled, tongue poking in the side of his cheek.

"Here you go," the waitress said, placing two latte mugs with hearts on top. She also placed a cream croissant between us with a wink toward Damon. "It's on the house."

"Thank you," we said politely in unison. Despite the obvious charm pointed in his direction, I couldn't find myself upset about gaining a free croissant in the process. Wow being an attractive male had its perks.

"Okay, I think I can do that," he agreed.

"Okay then, we have ourselves a deal." I took a sip of the delicious coffee. *Well hello. It looks like I've just found my new local coffee shop.*

My smile slowly dimmed as I tried to remind myself of my reasoning as to why I'd come to Manhattan. I hadn't told many people as to why I'd come here, or more specifically no one ever really asked. It seemed so long ago. "To put simply, being in Ithaca didn't make my heart sing. I've always wanted to be a travel columnist and there was more opportunity here." Plain and simple.

"And do you feel like your heart sings now?" he asked. The question took me by surprise. When was the last time I'd been able to think about it? Thoughtfully, I cut the cream croissant in half, realizing I hadn't eaten all day and the sweet temptation was tantalizing me.

Damon clasped his hands together and rested his chin on them as he looked at me intently. He prompted me to continue. It confused me how open I was with Damon and how easy and natural it felt. It was a vulnerability I wasn't acutely used to. But I supposed in his line of work, being so charismatic, he was used to retrieving answers.

"I'm living the dream now right, well all short of actually having the dream job." I tried to laugh it off, not quite ready to seriously ask myself that question. Wasn't I happy? "I'd always talked of traveling since I was a young girl. Running around the world and being a columnist. I wanted to accomplish it not only for myself, but for my father as well. He was so supportive of my writing career and I wanted to give it my all. So I packed my things and drove to the Big Apple. And well, here I am now," I said, taking a bite of the buttery pastry and almost melting into my chair with it. Damon was quiet, listening, watching, building a palpable tension between us.

"I lost my mother," Damon said cautiously, as if offering the slightest bit of intel would crumble his entire world. He struggled with the confession but without my encouragement he continued, upholding his half of our bargain. "From cancer. I admire your courage. I went the other way. With the family business, there was a lot of expectation for my sister and me to take over, to relieve my father from the pressure. He'd never quiet been the same after losing my mother. Before I knew it, we were it. The face of the company and tag-teaming every big decision. My sister's a complete control freak so she loves it. But then life threw a few more curveballs, and well, I think my absence has left her kind of pissed," he said with confused laughter. His eyebrows were furrowed as if he was unsure about how much he'd revealed. I wanted to ask more but knew that if I did, he'd retract immediately.

"I'm sorry for your loss" was all I managed to say. Losing a parent was never easy. And I wasn't sure what else had happened or the depth of his pressures, but I was grateful he'd finally, even if reluctantly, shared something with me. And I couldn't understand why that was so important to me.

"It just kind of sucks," he said lightheartedly. "Sorry, I don't want to make you uncomfortable."

"Don't apologize," I said, quickly reaching for his hand. He stared at me as he regained his composure, all emotions and vulnerability subsiding. His gaze dropped down to my hand on his. I retracted it instantly, taking a sip from my mug and stuffing my face with the last bite of my croissant half that immediately flaked everywhere.

He chuckled at my frightful response leaning over to wipe a napkin at my mouth. "You get embarrassed so easily. Have you never been with a man before Clover?"

I almost choked on the croissant as I swallowed. I was a shamble in the first place *because* of him.

"Of course I have." I swiped the napkin from him, realizing he was teasing me again. "Do you always tease your clients this much, I'm surprised you haven't run out of business."

"You're not my client right now," he condoned. Again, his gaze set alight a blaze through my body and my heart spiked an unnatural beat. I smoothed over my skirt, looking for a distraction. *Why was I so ridiculously attracted to this man?*

"Well, Mr. Charming, even amongst your teasing, you're certainly very thought-provoking." I downed the last of my hazelnut latte, saddened by its cold remains.

I found it confusing how easily I could talk to Damon. We'd only just met, and yet I felt like he was as familiar as a best friend I'd known since college.

"Thought-provoking is good. I've been called worse," he joked. He looked at his watch, I did the same, realizing we'd already been here for two hours.

"Should we go get your wallet?" I asked, collecting my things and preparing for the cool autumn air outside.

"Okay, and Clover, you can have the second half of the croissant," he said with a sly smile. "You've been eyeing it off ever since you cut it in two."

I smiled, not subtle in the slightest. "I accept your offer." And with an internal squeal of utter delight, I grabbed the second half to go.

Chapter 14

Damon

The moment Clover opened the door Pudding bolted through with a speed no cat that weight should be able to muster. She wedged him awkwardly between her leg and the doorframe, dimming his grand escape. The petulant cat let out a defeated, malicious noise.

"He's surprisingly quick for a chubby cat." Pudding's ears pulled back and a scornful almost humanlike glare pinned me. *He really didn't like being called chubby.* She swiftly collected him and hoisted him under her arm as she opened the door.

"I know, I swear he's the only reason I stay half in shape," she joked as she tried to blow the part of her fringe that fell into her eyes. "Come in."

She dumped Pudding on the couch as he

meowed impatiently, most likely waiting for his food. The wallet was exactly where I'd put it, seemingly untouched, and I felt reassured that she obviously hadn't gone through it. If she had, she could've easily found out who I was.

There was a sincerity about Clover that I felt magnetized toward. She treated me differently to anyone else I'd known. She wasn't a part of my world and felt like a cool fresh breeze and for the first time in a long time, I felt like I could breathe. Like the outside pressures amounted to nothing and didn't even cross my mind when I spent time with her. I didn't entirely understand the sensation, but I was grateful and amused by it all the same. A tug of guilt consumed me. *Was I being disingenuous to her?*

"Here," she offered me my wallet.

I brushed my thumb over her fingers as I collected it, curious by how she'd react. The immediate hot need for more grappled *me* stronger than her. Every curious wonder over her skin, no matter how delicate, demanded more. I paused my thumb on her fingers, attempting to regain control.

I wanted to explore Clover. And that was *dangerous*. She was frozen under my touch, those soft brown eyes unsure of where either of us wanted to take this. Would she let me have her? I stared at her lips in wonderment as to what she'd taste like. I considered how it'd feel to nip on that plump bottom lip and claim her as mine, to be entirely consumed by the heat this woman inflicted on me.

I pulled away my wallet slowly, our eyes never breaking contact. Her breath hitched, the tension palpable between us. And yet I engaged every spark of restraint. This was *dangerous* territory. "Thank you." My voice came out as a lust-hungry croak.

"You're welcome." Her own voice mirrored my own. My knuckles began turning white as I clutched tightly to the wallet for dear life. If I were to allow myself to be consumed by Clover, how would it feel? What would it do to me?

A startling and disheveled meow crept in between us. We both dropped our gazes, breaking the tension, onto the fat orange cat who stared between us skeptically.

"I should feed him," she nervously laughed and hurried into the kitchen. It was like a cold splash of water to the face, one I was grateful for. I was losing control. *What was I thinking?*

"I can see that." I smiled faintly, trying to clear my voice. "Thank you for this." I raised my wallet as if it were some kind of prize. I had to get out or there was no telling how long it'd be until I lost control again. I hurried for the door and then lingered as I recalled something. *This could be a mistake.* I looked back over my shoulder at her. *But I wasn't yet ready to entirely let her go.* "I could probably make myself available Friday evening."

"What?" she asked, looking over her shoulder as she scraped the remains of the cat food tin into Pudding's bowl. That red flush hadn't entirely yet disappeared. My body reacted at the sight. *I needed to calm down.*

"For the party, if you'd like to show your boss up one more time." I shrugged, trying to appear more casual than I felt. What if she said no? I'd never feared rejection by a woman in my life, but I suddenly felt in foreign territory. And besides, she was a *client.* I justified that she needed a hand with her boss, clutching to the excuse as tightly as I wish I'd been holding onto her only a minute ago. My body was still taut with tension. I was playing with fire and temptation, and yet I wasn't ready to leave without knowing I'd see her again.

"How much will it cost me?" she asked.

Just you. "Nothing," I said coolly. "Consider it my thanks for not selling this to a pawn shop or something like that." Was I, babbling?

Curtly, she nodded. "Okay," she agreed quietly.

I was making a fool of myself and for what? I needed to leave. I nodded. "Good night, Clover." Then I closed the door behind me. In the empty hallway, I stood stoic for a moment, trying to regain my composure. What was I doing? It took all my effort to take the first step, because all I wanted to do was claim her... and now.

Chapter 15

Clover

"I'm telling you, he has the hots for you!" Cassidy exclaimed while flirtatiously waving at the lunch boy as he sheepishly made his way to the elevator. We were sitting in the lunchroom. I couldn't remember the last time I'd actually made time for a break, but it was refreshing.

"I'm not sure, I mean do you think he pities me?"

Cassidy scoffed as she bit into a forkful of her Mediterranean salad. After she swallowed, she pointed the fork at me. "You, my friend, are in complete denial of when a boy actually likes a girl. You guys were oozing with chemistry and tension yesterday."

"But it's so weird. We hardly know each other," I argued and bit into my sandwich.

"Yea, that's kind of the point of dating." And then she smirked. "Oh wait, I forgot you were already *boyfriend* and *girlfriend*." I offered her an effective glance that had her throwing her head back and cackling. "All I'm going to say is I've dated *a lot* of guys. And if they're making the time for you, they're interested. Why don't you call your sister, I'm sure she'll agree with me."

"And tell her I hired an escort who's now agreed to pretend to be my boyfriend?" I scoffed. Although I knew Megan would lap up every detail, I wasn't ready to admit it to her. I felt pathetic but also exhilarated in my hopeful fantasy that maybe he did like me. But I also knew very little about him. "Speaking of dating how goes yours?"

Cassidy rolled her eyes dramatically. "Well, you know, boys are boys and I'm not having any luck. I'm starting to think I need to just escape into the wilderness and find me a big old lumberjack or something. Live a simple life and live from the land, you know?"

I almost choked on my next bite. "And miss out on all the glitz and glam of the city? My how you've suddenly changed," I teased.

She chuckled, pulling out her cell as it buzzed. She paled as the screen lit up with, "Do Not

Answer." She immediately hung up, pocketing the cell as if it burned her.

"Is everything okay?" I asked. I'd never seen Cassidy in a quiet fluster like that before.

"It's fine," she lied with a faint voice, followed by a bright smile.

"Clover," Debra interrupted, her pointed nose the only thing entering the lunchroom as if a closer proximity would sully her. "I need you in my office. *Now.*"

I looked at my half-eaten lunch and Cassidy who kicked up a fake smile. "I'm fine," she lied. "But you, my friend, not so much by the sounds of it. I'm cheerleading you on."

I did everything to resist rolling my eyes as I threw the remainder of my sandwich in the bin. I had the sense I wouldn't have an appetite after this conversation.

Debra was standing behind her desk, arms crossed as she looked out at the hustling city beyond. "What's this?" she asked, pointing to a two-page spread. I crossed the room and glanced at it briefly. *I should've known.*

"That's an article I recently wrote about a local hotspot in Manhattan. I wanted to pass it by the journalism department and ask their opinion on it."

"And what, expect to be published in the magazine or something?" she mockingly accused. "I didn't realize I paid your wage for you to focus on your own selfish desires."

"I wrote this in my own time," I gritted out.

"I don't care. Your focus should be on the tasks I assign to you and I won't stand for this underhanded game. You have a role and a responsibility to this magazine. I wonder if by being swept away by your new beau you're grasp and understanding in what that role encapsulates has been lost." She scoffed again, her gaze blazing furiously.

"Ten minutes ago, I received an email from one of our biggest clients, who have decidedly dropped us and their advertisement contract to shift over to *Be True* magazine. Were you not on top of this client?"

"I haven't yet seen that email, I—"

"I'm certainly not surprised especially if you're out chitchatting with the receptionist all the time. You need to fix this!"

I felt my taut nerves rising. With my back up, I stated simply and calmly, "Does not some responsibility lie on the marketing department for this also? I—"

"How like you to throw someone under the bus for your own short comings. *Fix this* or start looking for work elsewhere. I can't even stand to look at you right now. Get out of my sight," she waved me off.

All my rage bubbled to the surface, and I tried my best to elegantly walk out of her office before I completely exploded. I *needed* to keep this job. I wouldn't lose to her now.

"Clover," Cassidy called out to me as I hastened past her, tears prickling in my eyes and daring to escape. I just needed one second alone. Gratefully, no one else was in the bathroom. I sat on the seat, taming my hysterical breathing as tears streamed down my face. *I was so angry*.

I would not let her make me cry. I refused to give her that power over me. But I was just so furious. I never used to let her get to me, so why now? Everything felt like it was slowly falling apart and I had no idea how to help myself.

Chapter 16

Damon

"You seem awfully spirited today," Alex commented, rallying his notes for our meeting as we walked down the hallway.

"Do I have a reason not to be?" I said, side-eyeing him.

"If you leave your tardiness for another minute then perhaps," Michelle chastised as we walked into the boardroom. A handful of our developmental team was already waiting. Purposefully, I sat two seats up from my sister, forcing Alex and Sotiny to sit next to one another. He seemed hesitant as he pulled out his chair, offering me an unfavourable look. The icy chill between the two was palpable. I glanced briefly at Michelle who quirked an almost unnoticeable smile. Had I not known her my entire life, I wouldn't have noticed the subtle smugness. But because I did know her, I knew she would've done the same thing.

"Right, let's get into it. Congratulations to Alex's team for obtaining a huge client this week, Bewildered Jewelry." Everyone applauded Alex who was smugly smiling. His smile seemed to fall slightly as his gaze drifted over to Sotiny who offered a half-assed clap staring at her notes.

After a few more footnotes, Michelle handed the floor over to me. I hadn't created a PowerPoint or well-designed pitch. I hadn't voiced this idea or had the motivation to query and put it in action. But suddenly with a new wave of energy I wanted to hear their thoughts on it. I took to the front and adjusted the cuffs on my suit. Everyone's attention was on me as my sister took her seat at the end of the table.

"I've considered this idea in the past, but I think it's time we set our sights on exploring different avenues. I want to extend further into a sports-focused magazine, targeting mostly men. We can do a twelve-month trial and distribute amongst our two main offices here and Chicago. I want to offer more diversity to our readers."

Everyone in the room glanced at one another, most of them unreadable. "Seventy-one percent of our market is women, from a marketing perspective, I'd have to agree that attempting to reach the male audience is a bold and refreshing challenge," Alex added.

"Of course you would," Sotiny chimed. She seemed uncomfortable by the gazes that drifted to her. I noticed the freckles scattered across her nose, complementing the strawberry blonde of her hair and bold blue eyes. She looked fragile but from our few encounters she was far from.

"What do you mean, Sotiny?" Michelle elaborated.

"I agree that we should focus on the male market and sports is a great addition. But I think perhaps we should trial it on the online editions first. It's more reachable and I would consider bringing in someone high profile who's already within the industry."

"What like an athlete?" someone else asked. Despite her confliction with having to breathe the same air as Alex, she was a Harvard woman through and through and didn't mince her words or ideas. And with Michelle's encouragement, was outspoken with often productive outcomes.

"No, not an athlete. That just doesn't feel right.

What about a sports manager or something? Somebody who's built his success not in one field but encouraged and built many careers in different fields."

"That's not a bad idea, actually." Michelle nodded.

I agreed. We rounded the table, brainstorming. I felt alive creating something new again. I'd envisioned the expansion years ago, and yet somewhere along the way it vanished, most likely as I focused on the core growth of our business and running the day-to-day. It sparked a fire in my stomach again and I almost felt *hungry*.

"Okay we'll go over the finer material," Michelle concluded. "Sotiny and Alex, I want you two to work in conjunction with framing this. Damon, I'll let you champion the project."

The two flinched under their allocation and before either could dispute, Michelle gave them an effective glare. "Thank you for your work today, everyone." And with that, the meeting concluded. Everyone began to filter out, including Alex and Sotiny who were uncomfortably avoiding one another to find the exit.

Once everyone had left, Michelle closed the door behind them.

"You weren't kidding about those two, huh?" I said, loosening my tie. She silently watched me, crossing her arms in that intimidating way she'd often done, even when we were children and she wanted a toy or treat I had. "What?"

"What's this?" she asked waving her finger about me.

"What?" I asked, leaning against the back of the room beside the projector.

"You seem different. Two weeks ago you were all gloomy and didn't want to participate and now you're opening auction to new ideas."

"You wanted me to be more involved, didn't you?"

Her shoulders sagged slightly, tension rippling out of her. "You're not taking drugs or something are you?"

"What?" I said, exasperated.

"Because you know if you are I'll totally kick your ass, right?"

I kicked off the wall with a devilish smile, taunting her even further. "No thank you, if memory serves correctly, you always used to pull my hair."

She shrugged. "Well, I never said I fought fair and besides you were always a sore loser."

I brushed past her, stretching out to give her a

brief hug. "Everything's okay, Michelle," I reassured her. She flinched under my hug, a wave of guilt passing through me, considering how long it'd been since I'd properly thanked her. The last two years had felt like running through the motions. I'd been here, but not at the same time. And she'd maintained our business flawlessly. "Thank you."

I felt her gaze on my back as I left the room, only to face a sulking Alex who clutched onto his notes like a lectured schoolboy. *Looks like this new project was going to be his living hell but my new form of entertainment.*

Chapter 17

Clover

Marcial had already cried twice because of the heartfelt farewells and gifts he'd received. Friday crept up quickly and I was tired from the extra days I'd stayed back. I managed to organize the cafeteria into a classy function room of sorts, complete with champagne and decorated with silver and gold balloons. Not forgetting to mention the oversized cake that we'd now be eating for the next week.

Spirits were high as the sound of champagne bottles popping littered the room. It was a lively bunch that ran the *Candice Magazine*. Although we often had our differences and debated them quite freely, everyone compensated by drinking together happily, excessively even, when the company paid for it.

I was arranging some trays in the kitchen area when Cassidy bounced to my side with glass of champagne in hand. "You did a great job. I'm going to pretend this was for my birthday."

"You told me you didn't want me to organize anything for your birthday. And it was *you* who kicked me out of your celebratory drinks, remember?"

"And what a fantastic idea that was! I'm practically cupid. Speaking of, when's lover boy due to rock up?" she asked distractedly, before waving Issobelle over.

"I don't know, he said soon. And he's not a lover anything. And when did you and Issobelle become such good friends?"

"Whatever, Miss in Denial. And Issobelle's hilarious, I really like her. Have you spoken to your sister about him yet? I know how close you two are."

I took a sip of the champagne. "I honestly haven't had the time to call her over the last two weeks." And partially I was avoiding her. If anyone could sense something was up, it was her. And I didn't know exactly what I was feeling right now.

"My, my, my doesn't he look even more delicious

a second time round," Cassidy chimed as Damon walked in. "And you said you're not paying for him this time?"

"Can you please stop saying that," I shushed her, paranoid anyone would hear. She threw back her head laughing, carefree.

"Still rocking the dark shades, I see," Cassidy greeted. Damon inclined his head. "If I didn't know better, I'd start believing you didn't want anyone to discover who you truly are Mr. Damon." It created an awkward tension between us. Because it'd been something I'd been curious of since the moment I'd met him. I justified that many people in New York set on the new trends. But it didn't make it any less uncomfortable by the reality of him scarcely telling me much about who he was. "I'm going to hand Isso-belle one of these." She took another glass of cham-pagne and sauntered off.

"She's quite the character isn't she?" Damon said as she walked off. He leant over and kissed me on the cheek. It felt like lightening had struck as my entire body broke out in unfamiliar goose bumps. He whis-pered against my ear, his hot breath flushing down the side of my neck. "It's good to see you again, Angel Puff."

I could feel others' eyes on me, embarrassed by

my obvious reaction to him. But this of course was part of our agreement, and yet I really didn't understand what he was getting out of it. Perhaps some sick entertainment, but in my hearts of truth, I'd hoped for something much more. But the reality was, this would all eventually come crashing down. I'd caught myself in a web of lies, and yet as Damon pulled back from me, slight confusion in his gaze, I didn't want to pull away either.

"She always keeps us on our toes here." I offered him champagne with a charming smile.

Damon fit in swimmingly, and it was much to my own flattery that a lot of the models swarmed to him as he entertained them politely. But his gaze always flickered back over to me, reassuringly almost. People were drawn to him like moths to a flame and from the outside, I wondered again why he was even here with me. What weird situation had I gotten myself into?

A few glasses of champagne later, Cassidy, Issobelle and I leant against the kitchen counter casually. Gratefully, Debra had already left. Her brief conversation with Damon seemed to dissatisfy her. She gave Marcial a hug and present after a flamboyant speech and left, leaving me to feel like I could finally breathe and enjoy my time.

"He's a good boy that one," Issobelle chirped, plopping a cherry into her mouth.

"You're not meant to eat the stem," Cassidy reprimanded. The two had become close and it was nice to casually laze about talking about nonwork things with them.

Issobelle rolled her tongue around and swiftly presented a knotted stem. Cassidy's eyes grew wide. "Impressive," she encouraged.

Issobelle shrugged, though she held an element of smugness. "Your boy, he's a good one," she said again, pointing to Damon casually as she threw back another cherry. She'd confiscated the bowl off the communal table with no cares in the world for sharing.

"Isn't he just!" Cassidy beamed, casting a wicked smile in my direction. "He definitely holds that mysterious vibe to him though, doesn't he?"

"Well, it's still early days," I mused, not sure what else to say.

"I can't trust any men these days," Issobelle said nonchalantly, throwing another cherry into her mouth. She was watching over Damon and the hoard of women around him like some bemused entertainment. "Or women. They're all as bad as each other."

"You bi?" Cassidy asked curiously as she played with the bottom of her curls.

Issobelle shrugged. "Depends on the night." She smiled slyly. "I just couldn't be bothered with the dating scene. It just seems like people are always after something, you know? I'd just much rather focus on myself and my art form."

"It's a good way to be," I agreed. Although, I was starting to realize the consequence of throwing yourself in to work for too long. Damon was an unexpected fun. And it dawned on me how long it'd been since I'd done things that had no benefit to my career. He'd unknowingly begun forcing my eyes to open and... *play*.

"Yea, the last guy I dated stole one of my expensive watches after crashing at mine for the night, can you believe that?" Cassidy chided.

"Did you report him?" I asked.

"No, there's no point. It was a one-night stand. I didn't even know his last name. But if I see him on the street, I'd be sure to give him a piece of my mind."

"Cassidy, that doesn't sound okay, surely you can get footage of his face from your apartment building's security or something?" I was assuming she lived in an apartment building. Then again, I didn't know much about Cassidy outside of work either.

"It's fine. These things happen right? All in love and war or something like that," Cassidy brushed it off. It was my father's anyway, so I didn't really care." She took a mouthful of her drink. I wanted to ask more, but I paused, falling short. I didn't mean to pry. If she felt comfortable enough, she'd open up in her own time.

"What a prick" was all Issobelle said before throwing a handful of nuts into her mouth. I hadn't even noticed she'd swapped the bowls out. "I'm going out for a vape."

"I'll join," Cassidy hurriedly agreed as she began filling up our champagne glasses.

"Since when do you vape?" I asked, deciding whether I should have another glass. With my lack of sleep, it'd already gone straight to my head. But with the enthusiasm Cassidy was filling it, it didn't look like I had much of a choice.

"I don't vape, but I need to find myself busy elsewhere." She charmed a smile.

"I feel like I'm missing out on all the fun over here." Tingles straightened my spine as Damon stood behind me.

"Not at all, we were just about to leave actually

but here, have another one." Cassidy swapped out his empty glass for a new and generously poured one. "Have fun, kids." She waved goodbye and followed Issobelle.

"If I didn't know any better, I'd say your colleague's trying to get me drunk," Damon purred.

"You and I both." I raised my glass to cheers his. That crooked smile sent my heart into a flutter. I casually turned around to stack the bowls Issobelle had easily downed, distracting myself from his charm that seemed to work so effectively on me.

"I couldn't help but think you're avoiding me this evening?" Damon queried lazily as he leant over the bench to look at me.

"Avoid you?" I nervously laughed. "It's been my utter delight and honor to watch you captivate every being here tonight," I dryly joked. His intuition and ability to speak his mind was disconcerting. I was hoping he hadn't noticed. I *had* been avoiding him because every time I stared into those molten brown eyes, I was a spluttering mess.

"Ah, Clover," Lucas, head of the journo department, bounced over. I couldn't have been more grateful for his timing. He glanced over Damon briefly before readdressing me. "I loved your piece on Hotspot Manhattan. I suggested to Debra we post it on our online blog and see how it takes off. Maybe we can have you write a few regular pieces for us." He wiggled his eyebrows.

It felt like a bucket of ice had been poured over me. Involuntarily my jaw clenched. "Sorry?" I asked quietly confused. Had I heard him right? An unfamiliar anger lifted through my body.

He seemed confused. "Your piece that you gave to Sanderson, she gave it to me to look over. I suggested we post it. Has Debra not spoken to you about it yet?"

My throat closed up. He'd suggested it go further? And she shut me down. Without realizing, my grip had tightened on my glass. Damon's hand pressed on my lower back, momentarily bringing me back to the room. I could feel his concern through the subtle touch. *Calm.* I loosened my grip and tight jaw, grateful for his presence. I offered Lucas a curt smile. "We did speak about it." I tried to remove the disappointment and anger from my tone. "She advised that now might not be the right time to publish it."

I could feel Damon tentatively watching me. My stomach felt like it'd dropped through the floorboards. Of course she'd done this. How low was she truly willing to go to sabotage me?

"Oh that's such a shame, I really thought it was perfect but Debra knows what she's doing. I'd definitely be interested to see what other pieces you come up with, though if you'd keep me in mind?"

"Of course," I said with a tight smile, doing all I could to not shake and cry.

"Well enjoy the rest of the party. I better leave before the missus starts calling me or then I'm in trouble," he laughed though there was a glint of fear in his eye.

When Lucas left, Damon spoke. "Why didn't she approve of the article?"

"It just didn't fit," I said tersely, again trying not to burst into tears. Even through his darkened shades, I could sense his gaze had narrowed on me suspiciously. His hand burned on my lower back, filling me with an unsettled desire to just grab his lips and take all my frustrations out on him. And how stupid was that?

I tried to take a step back, to clear my head of this confusing intensity. I bumped into Marcial rummaging through the fridge and was knocked back. I automatically put my hand against Damon's hard chest to steady myself. Damon's reflexes were just as quick, and one hand settled on my hip. My face was now inches from his. Almost imperceptibly, his lips parted. I was dimly aware of his pulse beating rhythmically beneath my fingertips. After a long, intense pause, he looked down to where my champagne had colored a small spot on his shirt. He smiled easily, but I felt myself redden, realizing I'd spoiled his shirt.

"I'm so sorry," I blurted.

"Oh sorry, guys," Marcial said with a slur.

Damon charmed him with a smile. "It's fine." He grabbed my arm to steady me and stepped back to make sure I hadn't spilt any on myself. His deep dark-brown eyes seemed to swallow me as my heart raced. So many emotions wanted to overflow right now. His hand slid down my arm to my wrist, where he held it for a moment. I couldn't look away from him. It was only when I looked at his hand clasped around mine that he also seemed to notice his lingering touch and pulled away with a tentative smile.

What was that? I'd been with men before, but none had ever consumed me in such a way, creating a fire like no other through my whole body.

"Let me clean that for you," I said, flustered.

I turned to get a cloth, realizing it'd had cleaner days.

"Clover, it's fine," Damon said reassuringly.

"No, I'll clean it. I know, we'll get you a new shirt, it's fine," I said, dashing out of the room and toward the fashion department. Damon shouted after me, but I headed steadfast for it, his footsteps swiftly behind. I was a flustered mess.

Luckily, the room was still open and I found the men's section. *I'm sure he could borrow something and have it returned.* The room was dimly lit with multiple rows of clothing. Suddenly I wished I hadn't had so many glasses as I tried to rationalize my thoughts.

Damon caught my arm and spun me. "Clover, it's fine." His face slackened as small tears sprung in my eyes. With a fiery determination, I willed them away, not allowing Debra or whatever this was to get to me so badly. I was better than this, but I just felt so damn overwhelmed. "Clover?"

My bottom lip wobbled. I wanted to say that I was fine and sorry about his shirt. But I was too scared that if I opened my mouth, the croak of my voice would follow. I just stood there with a fiery determination not to cry in front of him. I felt like a deer in headlights but instead of looking at me with pity, he kissed me instead. And my entire mind went blank.

His lips crashed against mine, encouraging me to

open up to him more as his tongue brushed against mine, needing and wanting. My body acted on its own as I reciprocated, following his lead as he pushed me against the wall, a rack of clothes shaking against me.

My lower stomach heated as he raised my leg over his hip, as if needing all of me around him. I pulled him in closer with the same desire, my nails digging into the back of his neck and hair like a wild animal. I couldn't breathe. Didn't need it. I only needed him, all of him, filling me with exotic promise.

Our lips parted, my whole body shaking as I inhaled. I scanned his now stormy dark almost black molten eyes that told me everything that he desired.

Again, I was confused, I didn't understand. I wanted to know why? Why me?

As if in answer to hearing all the wild thoughts that were springing to mind, he declared with a rough and sex-laced voice, "I want you."

My breath hitched as every thought as to why I shouldn't came crashing into me. But I was tired of living cautiously with no fun. Even if it was for one night, surely, I was allowed to splurge. I wanted to *play*.

I licked my lips, my breath still finding rhythm.

"Would you like to come back to mine?" I asked far more meekly than I'd like it to have come out. But I hadn't invited a man to my bed in... for as long as I could remember and the uncomfortable squirm of rejection filled my mind.

But without words and a pinned stare he slowly nodded, right before he kissed me again—making his claim anew.

Chapter 18

Clover

I'd barely opened the apartment door when Damon pulled me closer. The elasticity of whatever control we'd been holding onto snapped. Light spilt into the room from the city's lights, shadowing our kisses.

"I'm sorry, Pudding," I mumbled through kisses as I ignored the meowing cat. Damon chuckled and lifted me around his hips. I clasped my gray work-pants around him like an anchor, flustered by the already apparent hard on he had.

"Sorry, buddy, but she's mine tonight," Damon breathed, his hand securely fastened underneath my ass, the other holding my neck in a firm, possessive grip.

"Room's that way!" I pointed, the slight sway of the room and excitement from the bubbles eliciting an extra buzz through me.

Damon kicked the bedroom door shut behind us, throwing me on the bed. I bounced, grateful for once that I'd had time to put away my laundry. A golden light streamed through my window above the bed and my breath hitched as Damon unbuttoned his shirt. *Was this really happening?*

The full-length mirror in my room reflected his muscular back as he stalked toward me. My mouth suddenly felt dry. I knew he was ridiculously attractive but this... this was next level. "Clover?" He growled, drawing my attention to him and not the reflection through the mirror. Those molten, dark-brown eyes were blazing with hot need.

I raised my hand, swirling it around in the direction of his chest area. Even the V line that cut into the edge of his pants was ridiculously prominent. The swell of his groin, promising all kinds of delight. *Did this man ever eat a donut?* "It's just a lot to take in," I breathed. A boyish grin spread across his face.

"And I could say the same for you," he growled. "Are you still sure, you're okay with this?" A flutter of vulnerability crossed his expression. I hoisted myself up onto my elbows and pulled him by the untouched tie around his neck.

His warmth wrapped around me and I sealed my lips on his by way of consent. My body danced in flames for him. Everywhere he touched left a trail of jitters, swarming my stomach with a flood slowly rising. Of course I was sure and I blocked out any thoughts that might counter otherwise.

His tongue rolled over mine, the low guttural groan from him naturally enticing my body to stretch upwards into his. He guided his hand under my shirt, cupping my breasts and pinching my nipples through the bra.

All of him was perfection. The lightly tanned skin, the messy hair, his intense gaze. But what was more delectable was the intensity and need to have one another. To solidify whatever this was, even if it was only ever meant to be one night of play. I flooded with a heated pulse, wanting every inch of him inside of me now.

As I began to unbutton my shirt, he leant back undoing his own belt and pants, the moment a tease in itself as we slowly undressed ourselves in front of one another, enjoying the view. I flung my shirt and pants to the floor and his eyes darkened. He reached for his tie, but I grabbed his hand to stop him. "Keep it on." Those eyes grew heavier as I took the liberty of pulling down his jocks. His heavy cock sprung free and my mouth watered. Considering I hadn't been with a man for almost two years, I was intimidated by its size, but it did nothing to deter my hunger and thirst.

I bopped down, dragging my nails down his thick thighs as I licked the tip of his shaft. The smooth texture ran a tingle down my spine as I greedily took it in my mouth. Damon groaned, again sparking another pool of warmth into the depths of my stomach. I took him in, enjoying each and every lick and suck. His hand coiled in my hair, enjoying my natural rhythm. It felt *so* good. Having him here, servicing him like this. A flutter in my stomach turned, reigniting a side of me I'd long forgotten. I moaned around his cock, eliciting his own primal noise.

"Clover." He tugged my hair and reluctantly, I released my grip, satisfied by the suction noise that sounded like a small pop. He feverishly kissed me, pulling me up to my knees and just below his eye level. His hands roamed with intent as his fingers found the curls to my opening. He circled my clit, the touch of him almost driving me crazy immediately. He watched me and the way that I reacted to him and was satisfied by the small pleas that escaped.

I stroked his cock, enjoying the meaty weight of it in my palm, noticing that tendril in his neck jutting out. He curled a finger inside of me, my tightness preparing to make room for him already. His finger pumped me as he relentlessly watched my every little whim, then inserted a second. I wanted to kiss him, but there was an intimacy far greater as I watched him, saw him in his glory. He was here with *me*.

Looking past his shoulder and into the full-length mirror, my entire body clenched and released around his two fingers. He thrusted deep, his palm cupping me every time. I could see everything from this angle, his muscular ass, his shoulder that shifted to work me into a puddle. My legs began to quiver. I clenched his cock, a hiss exerting from him as he tugged back my hair and leered down at me. His lips crushed mine, softly, deeply and sensually.

"I want you," he growled.

"I'm yours," I whispered back, my soft body molding to his rock-hard one. He growled approvingly.

"I want you on your back," Damon commanded. Slowly, I lay back, watching as he took a condom from his wallet and set it to the side. "Do you trust me?"

I was sprawled out in front of him, completely naked and his for the taking. "Yes," I whispered breathlessly.

"Good." He unfurled his tie and bound my hands to the headboard with efficient ease. The tie cut tightly around my wrists, igniting a dangerous spark inside of me. I'd never *played* like this with a man before.

"Damon, it's been a while for me. So..." I swallowed. "Go easy on me at the start."

His eyes had almost turned to black as he dipped down to press his lips against mine, his tongue encouraging me to dance. I squirmed under his touch, my body hot under the weight of his despite not yet touching.

A streaking light flashed across his face, reflecting the few beaded spots of perspiration. His finger lightly trailed down my forearm, goose bumps rising in its wake. I was entirely open to him, vulnerable, yet giddy all the same. I peered down at that weighted cock, still unsure as to how I was going to take him in.

"It's been a while for me too, Clover," he admitted. Our gazes locked, and that glimpse of vulnerability shadowed his expression. A warm comfort settled in my stomach.

His fingers began to trail down my entire body, forcing it to naturally arch everywhere his finger brushed over. He was painting me in memory, I realized. Intently watching me as his finger guided a fiery trail.

When he reached my thighs, he hoisted me up, the weight of my ass nothing as he brought my heat to his lips and wrapped my knees over his shoulder. His tongue was a wicked fury and I squirmed, pulling at the tied restraint, realizing now why it offered pleasure and trust all in the same. I was completely at his mercy.

His tongue dove deep, lapping me up as he drove harder into my folds. He then sucked on my clit, building up a long-forgotten tension as I moaned and felt myself pooling for him. He licked at every taste, torturing me as I writhed under him, uncontrollably shifting between total bliss and needing more.

"I need you," I breathlessly begged.

A playful smile stretched over his expression— extremely devilish looking as he looked at me between my legs.

"Well, I'm not done," he teased.

"Don't mess with me," I retorted, surprised by

my own primal need. He chuckled lowering my legs and leaning over to kiss me again. He cupped my face while his other hand reached to untie my restraint. The moment I was set free, I wrapped myself around him in earnest, wanting all of him.

He grabbed the condom from the side table, his tongue tangling with mine as I knotted my hands through his hair. The hand that cupped my face slowly trailed down my neck and between my breasts, hitching on my hips.

I looked past his shoulders, pleased to see the condom on. I widened my legs, feeling vulnerable and dirty all the same as he stared, bewildered and at a loss. I don't think I'd ever shown myself to someone else so openly.

He leant over me, tensing as he slowly rubbed himself between my folds, the pressure of him already invasive. He was slow and careful as he pushed in. It hurt as my body tried to stretch to his size.

He kissed me again, a gentle distraction as he pushed deep inside of me. I couldn't breathe, as I focused on accepting all of him, my hips naturally rolling against his for more. In and out, a slow torturous dance began as I wrapped my legs around him, slowly enjoying the pain he filled me with.

A husky moan escaped me as he pushed to the hilt inside of me. In every way, this felt right—Damon inside of me, perfuming me and kissing me. He was hard, rough and soft all at once, melting into me like I'd never felt with any other. It might've been only for one night, but I wanted to savor it. Tonight, he was mine, and with kisses, I conveyed my thanks.

Chapter 19

Damon

There was a strength and delicacy to Clover. Her boss was an absolute bitch, and yet I wondered why she stood for it. She was a strong and capable woman, able to get work anywhere so why had she allowed herself to feel backed into a corner like this?

Her gentle breath scattered goose bumps across my chest as I folded her into me, my finger tracing her arm. There was a warmth to holding her in my arms with the softness of her breasts pressed against me. She was in every way beautiful, and I pushed away any conflicting thoughts, embracing this moment—embracing her.

"Doesn't it ever make you mad?" I asked, wanting to fight on her behalf. No one had ever dared speak to me like that, but I realized that was a privilege being in my position and born into power.

"What?" she asked, despite her groggy tone, she was wide awake. Her finger ran small circles over my chest.

"Your boss." If the public found out about how the editor in chief acted at *Candice Magazine*, they'd have her head and part of me was tempted to let it leak. But then I'd only be undermining Clover's power in the process. And it wasn't my place to get involved; I was after all only her escort playing make-believe boyfriend.

"Sometimes," she admitted. "I'm not unsusceptible to anger. But also, I'm grateful. It's a high-paying job, it revolves me around good people and a place for network. And all I can think is surely, I'll be rewarded soon. Not by Debra," she scoffed. "But the right opportunity will come along so I can focus on my writing again and hopefully travel. I have bills to pay, I can't just run with my tail between my legs because my boss is a brooding villain."

"A *brooding villain*?" I laughed. Her slow smile had me holding her tighter, possessively even. A startling and scary notion. "What do you do to release that pent-up anger?"

Silence. She considered it as if the centre of my

chest was the most fascinating thing she'd seen in months. "I don't know. I just throw myself into work. I try not to linger on it I suppose."

I propped myself up, shuffling her with me. I looked at my wristwatch. It was three in the morning. The sun hadn't even begun to rise, and yet I felt like I had more energy than I'd had in a long time.

"Do you have somewhere else to be?" Clover inquired sarcastically with a raised eyebrow. She propped up on one shoulder, her hair deliciously wild. I cupped around the back of her neck possessively before I kissed her.

"Nowhere unless it has you naked beside me." My cock started twitching as she melted against me once again. "I want to take you somewhere," I growled fisting her hair. Because if I didn't leave this room soon, I'd never leave at all.

"Now?" She laughed through kisses.

"Now," I replied. "Put on your sweatpants."

She jerked back. "My sweatpants?"

"It'll get a little sweaty where I'm taking you."

She effortlessly rolled on top of me, straddling and enjoying the jerk of my cock on her ass. "But I'd rather be getting sweaty with you *here*." Her hair cascaded around her face, and I noticed small bruises marking her body where I'd unknowingly marked her as mine. She turned me into a savage but who was I to deny her?

"Can you make it quick, Angel Puff, we have somewhere to be," I said with an already half driven tone. The things this woman did to me.

"It depends how I'm feeling and of course how long you last, *Dear,*" she challenged, bending over to nip at my bottom lip. She muffled my complaints with her tongue, subduing my head back into the pillow as she grabbed my throbbing cock.

The sun had begun rising when we finally arrived at the boxing gym. Her hair was pulled up in a messy ponytail, bags under her eyes since we hadn't yet slept, and yet she oozed with a flawless glow. She wore a loose green sweatshirt and black leggings and stared about the place, fascinated. A handful of the usuals were already training.

"You didn't seem like the boxing type to me? Wait, are you secretly like part of some gang?" She stopped in her tracks, dead serious. "Because I've read books, you know?"

I couldn't help but cock my head back with a

confused smile. I hadn't told her much about myself, but did I really look like the mafia type? "No, Clover, I work behind a desk. Like most New Yorkers." Tension rippled from her body as I reached out for her hand.

"Nice outfit," Terry, one of the owners walked past and winked. I was dishevelled with my suit pants and shirt from the night before. Stain and all. But in this moment, I really didn't care. And no one was going to tell me twice considering the generous donations and advertisement I did for them.

Clover gawked at Terry as he walked past. He briefly scanned over her, looking between us curiously but didn't say anything. I'd never brought anyone here. It was only ever Alex and me. But I wanted to show her this place, somewhere she could physically exert that pent-up frustration. It had in so many ways helped me and although it didn't have to be this gym, I wanted to help her in some way.

"That was one of the biggest guys I've ever seen in my life," she whispered sheepishly. I chuckled. Well Terry was a body builder and dual owner the boxing gym with his brother, Lorance as well as a local coach for both boxers and body builders.

"This way." As expected, the ring that was reserved for Alex and me was empty. Being a

Saturday morning though, I doubted Alex would even be in, he was no doubt still partying on some rooftop somewhere watching the sun rise with a new woman for the day.

Clover seemed to shy away from it. "You want us to spar?" she asked cryptically.

I slipped into the ring, adjusting the handheld pads. "No, I want you to let out some of that frustration." Despite her hesitation, she followed through.

"But isn't that what I was using you for only an hour ago?"

I raised an eyebrow, surprised by her tongue in cheek. I helped her into the ring and kissed her as passionately as I had only an hour ago. I pulled away with a smile, her eyes still closed as she was leaning in. How had I been able to resist this woman for so damn long?

She propped a hand on her hip. "And this is just all magically set up for us?" she asked, again skeptically, noticing that the rest were being used.

"You still really aren't a romantic, are you?" I teased.

"Is this your definition of wooing a lady? Bringing her out for exercise?" she asked as she grabbed the boxing gloves and strapped them over her wrists with delicate precision.

"I could say the same about coaxing a man into a workplace closet," I replied. Her cheeks immediately brightened red. A chuckle escaped again. Everything about her made me feel alive. Even now, the spontaneousness of bringing her here. I was elated to take us out of our mundane lives; ecstatic to take her somewhere new and draw more of this playful Clover out.

"Have you ever done this before?" I asked as she pretended to gage my stance.

"Me and my sister used to take classes. She's always been into sports and dragging me here, there and everywhere to try something new."

"Sounds like fun." I raised the pads to eye level, encouraging her to hit.

"It was." She smiled as if recalling those memories.

"Remind me not to mess with you or your sister," I teased. She laughed before stepping closer.

"This is one of the most random things I've done on a Saturday morning sleep deprived," she said before forfeiting to the moment and taking her first strike. Even watching her work out was sexy. And I was suddenly aware that my cunning plan was more torturous than I'd intended. The way her muscles flexed, and those curves. I was acting like a twenty-year-old—only able to think with one thing.

"Do you come here regularly?" she asked through sharp breaths, almost falling into a rhythm. It was surprising to see her in this setting and how naturally she was able to adapt. My little coiled Clover, who only worked, was seeing what other little bits and pieces this city had to offer.

"I only started coming a few months ago and found it helped me with work and my stresses. So now I come most mornings."

"So you're an early riser?" she asked as we circled one another.

"What made you think that I wasn't?" I asked regretfully. The moment I did, she seemed to sink back into her shell.

"Well since, you know, for your work, some of the events must be late."

I could immediately feel us drifting apart again. That rift opened the moment I was reminded about my lack of forthcoming with my identity.

"I don't take that many clients on, Clover. You were the first person in months."

Her soft brown eyes assessed mine, as if I might've been lying. "Do you often... you know, sleep with your clients?" she forced out.

"No," I adamantly said. "No. I'm not like that. This..." I pointed between us unsure of how to explain myself. I didn't know what this was between us. But what I did know was that I'd never wanted someone as badly as I wanted her. "This is not the normal. You're not the normal."

"Wow," she said teasingly, trying to make light of the seriousness of the situation, and I was relieved. I didn't know what answers to give her. This could only be what it was—some fun and exploring this unquenchable hunger we had for each other.

She slinked out of the ring, grabbing a bottle of water that one of the workers set aside for us. She ungloved herself. I followed her, grabbing the second water. "And you think *I'm* not normal. But *you* take a girl to have a workout session after sex?"

I laughed, my stomach hurting. "When you put it like that, why did you even follow me?"

"You said I'd like it," she joked, crossing her arms with a childish pout. But I knew very well all the things I could do to Clover to make her *like* it. I swept her over my shoulder knocking a small squeal from her. She kicked and punched back and forth. And despite the onlookers, no one said anything, ignoring our closed-off section that only the owner used and I hired out.

"You *will* like it," I growled.

"Damon, put me down," she said, embarrassed.

I stormed toward the private showers.

It was a small cubicle in the corner of a private room. I placed her back on her feet and locked the door behind us.

Her chest rose and fell. "No?" she asked unsure.

"No?" I queried. Her back was pressed up against the wall as I cornered her. Everything about her had me on edge. I had every intention of burning every inch of her into my mind.

"What are you doing next weekend?" I asked. Not able to think about when this day would come to an end. Was it too selfish of me to ask her? To want to show her more?

She was breathless as she tried to refocus. "Why?"

"I want to take you somewhere."

"Last time you said that we ended up at a boxing gym," she toyed as our lips teasingly brushed over one another's.

"Somewhere else, another surprise." I kissed her, almost desperately, a foreign shudder running through me, scared she might say no.

As if feeling my sense of urgency, she breathed out, "Okay."

Clover curled her fingers through my hair, rising on her tiptoes. With her other hand she grabbed my collared shirt and hungrily pulled me in. I had her against the wall, my cock throbbing as I slipped my hand into her leggings and furled my fingers into the small coils of her hair. She reefed off my top as I dipped one finger inside of her. Her sharp hiss and nip of my lip, jolting my already rock-hard cock.

She pushed me away, relinquishing my hold and tore her leggings off. I turned the shower on, shrugging off my pants to let my cock spring free. She went to grab my girth, but I stopped her, tugging her under the water and circling my fingers on her clit. The water trickled down her body, guiding me from her mouth, to her neck where I sucked, down to her nipple as I nipped and tugged at it. I slipped another finger into her, guiding my other hand around her hips and cupping her ass.

She was every bit mine, designed for my hands to explore. I dropped to my knees and buried my face into her folds. I drove my tongue between her lips with the water raking over my face as my cock stood to attention, craving to be inside of her.

"Shit, Damon," she breathed, her hands curling into my wet hair as she arched into me. I never wanted to stop exploring her. I wasn't ready for this to end.

No one batted an eyelid as we left in our coats with wet hair. I explored every inch of her and still hadn't had my fill. Despite how much we couldn't get enough of one another, we were both reaching our limits. Sleep sounded like a good thing about now.

"Damon?"

"Alex?" My head jerked back, peering at a very sober Alex midmorning as we left the boxing gym.

Alex looked between me and Clover, a dimpled grin forming. "And who do we have here?"

"Clover," she introduced herself and shook his hand. He grabbed it way too willingly for my liking, stirring me like always.

"I thought you'd be out drinking?" I asked trying to block his view and interest in Clover.

"Well, we're all full of surprises aren't we, my friend. Did he just take you to check out the gym?" he asked Clover curiously.

She nodded. "And here I thought I'd get coffee

instead," she joked, teasing me.

Alex's smile grew wider. "I like her."

"We're leaving," I grabbed Clover's hand to hurry us along. The less time Alex had with her the better. Not only was he a charmer but he could let anything slip.

"You two enjoy your, ah, date." He charmed another dimpled smile, purposefully peering around my shoulder and winking at Clover as we walked away.

He threw his head back and laughed at my reaction. He wasn't meant to see her. He'd do nothing but ask questions now. I felt childish, only wanting her for myself and although I trusted him with my life, I didn't want his interest directed toward her.

"A friend of yours?"

I couldn't tell her he worked for me. "More of a sparring buddy." We did after all debate almost every day.

"I'll grab you a cab," I promised Clover calling a yellow one down. "So, are we still on for next weekend?"

The cab pulled up beside us. She nodded. "Yea, although should I be nervous?"

I leant in and kissed her swollen lips, still not entirely ready to release her. "Always."

Chapter 20

Clover

Sunday morning I sat in front of the coffee shop Cassidy and I agreed to meet at. She was running ten minutes late which I didn't mind with a coffee in hand. I was nervous but excited to shop for a new bikini set. I didn't know where Damon was taking me, but he sent a follow-up text to make sure I brought bikinis and my passport. I'd been laying low at work all week and despite my disgruntlement with Debra, I'd been in a rather chipper mood.

She was the only person I felt like I could talk to about it. I knew it couldn't last forever, but I wasn't ready to call it quits yet.

"I'm *so* sorry, crazy story I'll have to tell you some other time," Cassidy said with a smile as she pointed to the second coffee in my hand. "Is that for me?" she asked coyly, appreciating the first sip. Cassidy looked flawless and like she'd just stepped out of a magazine.

"I was surprised you were able to come at short notice," I admitted as we started walking through Fifth Avenue. Cassidy's eyes glittered over all the stores.

"And miss the opportunity to hear what happened Friday night? Someone spotted you two leaving and I want the goss!" she squealed. "And besides my date canceled on me before I could cancel on them," she laughed. "I wouldn't miss this for the world."

Cassidy seemed to fill her spare time with dates and I wasn't sure whether I should be alarmed or impressed by her youthful take on dating in Manhattan. Now that I'd had a sliver of taste with Damon and that enjoyment, I wondered if I'd been missing out all this time. Or maybe it was simply because it was him.

"Well?" she encouraged. "OMG! You slept with him!"

"How do you know that?" I stuttered.

She jumped up and down squealing, drawing very little attention to us in the heart of New York. "I knew it! You guys were oozing with sexual tension all night. That brooding glare he'd give you even when surrounded by a swarm of models. He's totally into you. OMG How was it?"

"Sssh," I urged her with a smile, giddy in the same way that she was. I wrapped my arm around hers, tugging her into a store.

"Well, I spilt champagne on his shirt and tried to get him a new one from the fashion department."

She nodded quickly, absorbing every drop in suspense.

"And then he kissed me in the closet and we went back to my place."

Cassidy squealed again in the store jumping up and down in circles. This time the clerk did look our way.

"Sssh," I said again, embarrassed.

"This one," Cassidy said, grabbing a moss green two-piece off the rack and handing it to me for assessment. "Ooh and this." It was a glittery one-piece that had me sneering. "Trust me." I was shocked to find she'd picked my size correctly. "And was it amazeballs?"

The clerk came and collected the two garments Cassidy already decidedly put aside for me. She pinned me with a stare and I went bright red. "Don't start jumping up and down again." I grabbed her before she could break into hysterics. "But I don't know what to think because he took me to this boxing gym afterwards and then asked if I was free next weekend."

"What? Like where people box each other?" she asked.

I laughed as I slid into the changeroom, opting for the two-piece to try on first. I hadn't worn a bikini in as long as I could remember. "Yes as in where people box. He said it helped him with his stress and frustrations."

"I find that weird but endearing at the same time. Did he take you so you could fake punch the lights out of Debra?"

"Cassidy!" I reprimanded.

"What? She's a bitch to you. Okay so he's taking you somewhere where you need bikinis?"

"And a passport."

Cassidy popped her head through the curtain. I covered myself self-consciously. "A passport?"

"Yes. And get out," I lightly laughed pushing her back out.

"If it were anyone else, I'd be telling you he's going to kidnap you but in this case, he might be proposing."

I opened the curtain. "Ha, ha. Very funny."

Cassidy's jaw dropped. "Damn, Clover, you should be in a bikini more often. You might not have to work for your money then."

"I never realized how crude you were," I joked.

"Or hilarious I am." She threw back some curls. "And also, I think Issobelle's been rubbing off on me slightly. So do you know where you're going?"

"Not a clue."

"Ooh and the mystery continues," she said, then drumrolled.

I twisted back and forth, assessing myself seriously in a way I hadn't for so long. My Latino skin seemed dull from being in the office for so long. But for the most part, I still ate healthily and kept up a regular exercise routine. I loved the bikini set though. Cassidy had a really good eye for these things.

"So, what's the problem then?" she asked. I stepped back into the changing room, not sure on her second choice however.

"It's just a weird situation. I don't know how to feel about it. I'm clearly attracted to him. But I don't know if I should feel a certain way considering how we met. What if he treats all of his clients like this?"

"You think that the person you paid to escort you, who is now taking you somewhere payment free and footing the bill, is in it just for the money?" Cassidy asked.

I hated to admit it but she had a point. But what else was I meant to make of it all? I walked out in the one-piece and again Cassidy's jaw dropped. "Damn I have good taste."

"I could say the same for the price tag," I rolled my eyes. Again, I assessed myself, surprised by its flattering appearance.

"Well price tag is irrelevant when you're trying to lock them in," Cassidy said, throwing some curls over her shoulder.

"I'm not trying to lock anything in. This is just for some fun."

"Call it what you want, as long as you're enjoying yourself and he treats you nicely. Aaaaand it's a bonus that he's superhot. You know, hidden identity and all aside."

"Yea," I drawled out, the hidden mystery starting to get the better of me. But I went into this knowing it would only be fun. I couldn't get hung up on the smaller details.

Cassidy clapped her hands together. "Chop chop, we have more shops to visit."

"More? I only came for bikinis," I said surprised.

Cassidy looked appalled. "Nobody ever comes to

Fifth Avenue for *only* one thing. You've clearly never shopped with *me* before." A wicked smile crept over her, and I was suddenly terrified for the day ahead.

My phone vibrated in my pocket during the cab drive on the way home. *SHE-WOLF SISTER* lit up on the screen. I smiled at her self-proclaimed nickname. Sporty yes, a she-wolf, maybe not so much.

"Oh wow, look at that she finally answers!" Megan screamed through the phone. "Mom! She's alive and hasn't abandoned us yet!"

"Oh shut up." I smiled. "And tell Mom I said hi."

"You can tell her yourself. Wait, Mom—"

Over a squabbled commotion, Megan's cell phone was confiscated off her. "Clover, when are you coming back for a break? Megan told me your boss won't let you have her birthday off. Ooh I want to give her a piece of my mind."

"Yes, Mom," Megan teased her in the background.

I sagged in apology. "I'm sorry, it's been pretty

hectic at the office, but I hope to come back for a weekend soon maybe."

"Mom, give me that." I could hear Megan slapping away my mother. "You're guilting her again. Stop it."

"I'm not guilting her," my mother said defensively. "I'm just worried about her health. She doesn't have any fun anymore. She's a beautiful woman and should be living her life, not being crushed under the boot of her boss."

I chuckled despite the truth of it as I watched streets go by. Halting at a set of red lights, I watched everyone go about their day.

"Mom!" Megan exclaimed with a laugh. "Go bake a cake or something."

I could hear Mom mumbling under her breath, bringing a smile to my face. I could just imagine her baking and seething over a batter mix like it was her cauldron. My heart swelled as I thought of home. I missed them so much.

"That woman's nuts," Megan laughed. "But she's right. Your boss is a bitch."

"I know," I breathed. "And I *am* sorry."

"You know I don't care. I'm just worried about you. We miss you, Cloves."

"I miss you guys too," I sombrely admitted. "And how are the boys going?"

"Oh gosh, they're getting bigger by the day. There such a handful," she laughed. They were her pride and joy. And I had no doubt they were growing up to be handfuls because no one was rougher than Megan herself.

"And what about you? I hope you're taking some time out of work. You know you don't have to keep sending us money, Cloves. We're just fine here. We're worried about you."

I nibbled on my bottom lip. It was part of my pride being able to send them money and pay off the last of the mortgage. And although I knew they didn't need it, I felt like I was contributing to the household still. While Dad wasn't there, I wanted to make sure they could enjoy themselves, especially when I didn't need the money. And that wasn't to say I didn't have savings, I'd just rather spend it on them.

"I know. And I am getting out and doing things. I'm not that pathetic," I lied.

"Oh really? What's something you've done recently for yourself?" A smile spread over my face. *Many wicked things.* I wanted to tell her about Damon, but how could I, what would I say? This bubble would all be over soon anyway. "I'm actually going away this weekend with a friend. You know getting out of the city and stuff."

"Really, where to?" Megan asked inquisitively. "And with who?"

My heart leapt out of my chest as we slowly drove past the little coffee shop Damon had taken me to. My stomach twisted into knots at the sight of Damon having coffee with a beautiful woman with long black hair. Was he... escorting someone? To the same place he'd taken me.

"Clover?" Megan asked through the phone. I looked away from the coffee shop, disbelieving. I mean honestly what was I expecting?

"Hey, Megan, sorry to cut this short but I've just arrived at my destination. Do you mind if I call you back."

"Yea that's fine, just make sure you do," she said quietly on the other end. I felt terrible for hanging up on her, but my head had begun to swirl into a spiralling mess. How could I be so stupid? *He was an escort. I had no right to be jealous. Or did I?*

But I couldn't help but feel how I did, and that was the most terrifying part of the situation.

Chapter 21

Damon

"And you're not going to say anything about the bombshell brunette I spotted you with on Saturday? I knew something was up with you, I knew it." Alex pointed at me, licking his lips in victory, that cocky dimple forming.

I chewed on the inside of my lip, sitting behind my desk with arms crossed. He was the last person I wanted to know about Clover for this exact reason.

"You were holding out on me this whole time! Who is she? When did this start?"

"Firstly, I'm paying you for this hour right now," I reminded him.

His smile widened. "Oooh a little touchy are we?"

"Secondly, there's nothing to talk about and you're not to tell anyone."

"Well, I can't tell anyone unless there's something to tell," he goaded. "And you know your little secret is safe with me."

There was a light tap on my door and I was grateful for the break in interrogation. Alex was relentless when he put his mind to something—especially gossip. For the third time this morning, I looked at the phone in my side drawer. She hadn't replied since Sunday morning. I closed it again, reminding myself that she was a busy woman too. And yet I couldn't help but harbor an unsettled feeling in my stomach.

"Come in," I motioned.

Sotiny walked in, her gaze landing on Alex immediately. "I assumed you were here when I couldn't find you working in your office."

"We were just having a meeting," Alex lied as he readjusted his shirt self-consciously. I sat back, leaning away from their palpable tension. There was definitely history between these two.

"Well, that's convenient because I needed to speak with you both. I created a list of possible candidates you might enjoy looking through for the sports edition."

"I thought we were going to go over that together?" Alex begrudged.

"We are. Now. I printed you some copies too. I sent you an email Saturday night, but I doubt you had time to open them."

"Some of us go out on weekends and live a little," he jibed back.

"I suppose anything that ends in the word 'day' is reason for you enough, huh?" she replied dryly.

I stared between the two as if watching some ping-pong match. If it had been anyone else, I would've involved myself. But this was Alex's problem. Whatever beef they had, I'd let him deal with it.

"Thank you for this, Sotiny, I'll brief over them," I added when Alex was lost for words.

She seemed to realize I was in the room again, as her and Alex defiantly looked away from one another. It was almost laughable. I'd never seen anyone throw it back in Alex's face so hard. He was so used to using his charm on women that it was refreshing to see someone who was seemingly repulsed by the idea.

"Also, Michelle would like to see you when you're available next," Sotiny added. She was such a matter-of-fact woman, completely opposite to Alex.

"Thank you, Sotiny." With a brief nod of acknowledgment, she left the room.

"That woman drives me crazy," Alex growled, looking at the ceiling with a scowl.

"Did something happen between you two?" I asked.

He looked dejected as he hunched over the chair collecting his coffee. "Let's promise each other to not ask questions." He winked. "And I really wish this coffee had something stronger in it right about now. I'll see you around."

I was almost grateful to Sotiny icing over the room just to flush Alex out. I didn't want anyone asking questions about Clover. For the fourth time, I opened my drawer, peering down to the undisturbed cell. *Why hadn't she yet messaged?*

Chapter 22

Clover

I'd found myself every morning and night throwing on my sweatpants and running around the block with my headphones in. I just wanted to run, shaking off or running away from my disappointment. I hadn't replied to Damon's last message. I didn't know what to say or how to shape it. It had to stop where it was.

Yes, we shared an incredible night together, but I'd decided to let the fantasy stay at that. What did I expect dating an escort? That was the reality, although I knew that my feelings deluded themselves with something entirely different.

I slept restlessly and couldn't focus on work. So instead, for the first time in months, I picked up a

Jane Austen book, my favourite classic and revisited Mr. Darcy last night.

I was now sitting two hours early in my office Friday morning, going over today's agenda. The reality was slowly dawning on me as I stared at my wall clock. Was my work the only thing I really had to show for in my life? This last month had been a whirlwind, and I wasn't even sure what I was doing anymore.

Colleagues slowly ventured in and Cassidy was sending me worried glances through the glass walls of my office. I'd told her briefly about what I'd seen that Sunday afternoon and although she suggested that surely there was an explanation for it, I didn't want to hear it. It was the catapult I needed back into reality.

I made my way to the coffee machine in the cafeteria. No one else was in the room, which felt like somewhat a relief; I wasn't in the mood for chit chat today. With coffee in hand, I moved to the large windows at the back of the room, sighing heavily as I watched the hustle of the city beneath me. I'd been so sure this was the right place for me. But maybe it was time for a change of scenery. *Was that really how I felt?*

"Clover." Damon's voice startled me from the

doorway. My body sparked with tingles and my stomach dropped. *What was he doing here?* I turned and immediately dropped my gaze to the floor, unwilling to look at him and be sucked in to the magnetizing pull he had over me. He was wearing his usual dark shades, reminding me of his mysterious identity. I sensed Cassidy leaning over her counter, watching in suspense. I had to be strong and apply boundaries. That's why I wasn't returning his calls, right?

"You can't just rock up at my office. I'm working and I don't want to be called into Debra's office because of it," I said as coldly as possible.

"Yes, but you also didn't give me much of a choice when you didn't answer my texts or calls."

Had I the nonchalant attitude of Issobelle, I might've dared shrug and say, "Wasn't it self-explanatory?" But when I stole a glance his way, betraying myself, I couldn't cultivate such a distant response. I felt crazy. I'd only spent one night with him, and yet I felt like a fever was washing over me every time I faced him.

Though I felt childish in my feelings, I couldn't help but be serious in my conviction. I was taken aback that he had the nerve to still expect me to join him this weekend. I thought that maybe our flirtation and fun had piqued his interest as well. But now I realized that was just me and my wild thoughts. "I saw you with a woman," I said. "A client... at the coffee place you took *me* to. I don't really care. It is after all the line of work you're in. I just realized it felt strange to go on a weekend getaway with my escort, you know?" My tone was hushed so only he could hear me. I felt small and vindictive saying it out loud. A tiny part of me was hopeful that he had feelings for me in the slightest, so I didn't feel like it was all make-believe. And that was the very same notion that got me in this guttural feeling now.

He studied me for a moment, somewhat flabbergasted. At first, I thought he might've been angry. He placed his hands in his pockets and dipped his head, exhaling heavily. "I'm sorry, I should've explained myself better. Clover, I'm not taking on other clients. I took my sister to that café because she hadn't been since we were kids. My mother used to take us there as children but after she passed we'd never remembered its address."

"What?" I said, now embarrassed by my accusation. My forwardness had bitten me in the ass. Then I grew suspicious. *But how did I know it wasn't a cover-up?* I furrowed my eyebrows in confusion. I was a twenty-eight-year-old woman, yet I fluttered around him as if he were my first love. I was sensitive to his every gesture and word, and I felt unfairly powerless against him.

"That was my sister. I'm sorry if I'd known you'd seen us, I would've properly explained."

I stared at him for a moment, resting my hand on the window ledge behind me. I looked into my mug mortified. I shouldn't have said anything, maybe I should've just said I was busy. Why did I even care? It's not like he was mine; we had only just met. But it still didn't excuse my accusation toward him, especially on what was once a nurturing memory of his deceased mother. "I'm sorry," I said. "What an idiot I must look." I realized I said that last part out loud. I really wasn't making this situation any better for myself.

"You could've just asked me," Damon replied. "I'm a bit hurt that you'd think of me like that."

It was complicated to say the least. But wasn't it obvious, I was uncertain because he was after all an escort. But he genuinely seemed hurt. I was still so confused as to where I stood with him. But surely, by him standing in my office building now, was that not notion enough to display that he was interested? And so was I. But somehow, without even trying, I was ruining it.

"You're right, and I'm sorry, I just... I don't know what to think around you," I blurted honestly. After I said it, I shook my head and laughed at myself. "That's really embarrassing." Why was I a flustered mess around him?

"That's not embarrassing, Clover. To be honest, I'm surprised I came here after you stood me up. I kind of just ended up here," he said as he looked at the elevator. Behind him, I saw Cassidy shamelessly watching on, even though she probably couldn't hear a word we were saying. When Damon looked at her, she ducked quickly, as if minding her own business. He turned to me, and we both stood in uneasy silence, both uncertain. When we first met, we joked and teased one another. Now we were revealing a far more vulnerable side that suited neither of us.

"Are you still free this weekend? I know it seems complicated and if you don't want to go, then I'll leave and you'll never hear from me again. I just wanted to make amends if I'd stepped over a boundary and disrespected you."

"I don't regret what happened that night," I said quickly. *It was the first time I'd felt alive in... years.* But maybe that's why such a small matter shook me so greatly. It felt like I was playing with fire.

"I thought you might've. I know the circumstance we met under were strange, but I am genuine about you. I would like to take you away this weekend. But if we're past that stage, then I'm sorry."

"You're not mad at me?" I asked inquisitively.

"To be honest, I was. But I'm glad we spoke about it because I can understand it. If only it'd been sooner, so it wasn't playing on my mind all week. Poor Alex was like a punching sack at the boxing gym."

I inevitably laughed, a swell of relief easing through my body. His face softened. "I don't chase women on the other side of Manhattan, Clover. I can't and won't promise you anything, but I think we both deserve a small break from the city. And I enjoy spending time with you. Especially when you're naked."

My cheeks flushed red. My lower region swarmed with butterflies at the thought of our compromised position last time in the shower.

"Can you think of this weekend as my way as apologizing?" he asked.

"I'm the one that should apologize."

"Can we agree we both screwed up?"

I hesitated, my heart fluttering all over again. This man had a spell over me. But was I in any position to deny him? Was I even strong enough for that?

"Okay," I agreed quietly, that small sparkle of hope revisiting and betraying a part of me that wanted to be naturally guarded around this man.

His face lightened as he smiled, somewhat relieved. "Oh, Pookie, that makes me so happy," he jokingly mocked.

"*No* pet names," I snapped with a relieved smile in return, the tension rippling away. All I knew for certain was Damon was dangerous territory for me, because this unsuspecting bud of passion was leading me into a dead end and I was finding it hard to say no.

Chapter 23

Damon

"You do realize it's five thirty in the morning," Clover said by way of greeting as she opened her apartment door. I crossed my arms, mirroring the same mock stance. Her hair was still damp and a fresh fragrance perfumed her. She'd evidently only just had a shower. I ground my jaw. *No.* We had a schedule. I couldn't let my thoughts drift to other things, no matter how tempting.

"I didn't want you attempting another runner, so I took precautionary measures." I charmed a crooked smile. I brushed past her, pressing a kiss to her cheek, almost grateful that she'd agreed to come this week-end, even after our miscommunication. It was beyond me as to why I was so desperate to have her come. I hadn't done anything for a woman since...

I stopped my train of thought. Clover wasn't *her*.

"You can't really be like this first thing in the morning as well," she said, sweeping her hair into a ponytail—one that I wanted to wrap my fingers around and fist. I watched Clover dance about her apartment, packing last-minute things. She was dressed in tight jeans and a loose gray shirt. And all I could think about was what lay underneath. My grip tightened on the kitchen counter. *I needed to get a hold of myself.*

"I'm just naturally charming," I replied. "Ahh speaking of charming." I bundled Pudding, surprised that the cat had taken a liking to me. He must've been recently fed since he lazily tolerated me scratching his neck and behind the ear.

"You think he's charming until you have to sleep with him all night. He takes up the whole bed," Clover said as she rolled her neck around uncomfortably. "Right, all packed and ready to go." She stood triumphant with her small overnight bag.

The tension in the elevator was palpable, especially when she licked her lips in that way she often did, unsure as to what to say and slightly nervous. We purposefully stood on either side, as if any closer and we wouldn't be able to keep our hands off each other.

Clover readjusted her coat when the chilly air and early bustle of New York hit us. Allen stepped out from the driver's seat and collected her bag.

"Good morning," he greeted her with a friendly smile. Clover politely greeted him and I knew she probably recognized both Allen and the car, though she asked no questions. Allen's curiosity was certainly piqued but he very rarely asked about my personal affairs. Before coming here, I'd told him that he wasn't to speak of it, especially if my sister tried to swindle answers from him. He'd worked for my family for over a decade now and Michelle had found ways to force secrets out of him before.

I opened the door for Clover, bemused by her cool composure although I could see that clever calculation in her eye. The fewer questions she asked the better. Clover admired the dark leather interior. And without instruction, Allen pulled us into the early morning hustle of Manhattan and toward the airport. I felt Clover's skeptical gaze.

"What is it, Clover?" I asked nonchalant, resting my elbow on the leather armrest with a closed fist to prop my head up.

"Remind me who you are again? It seems like

you're not quite the humble escort you pretend to be. You probably never even needed my money to pay for your services in the first place," she scoffed. I looked through the front mirror where Allen and I locked eyes. He'd taken me to many of my escapades. He was one of few who knew about my dirty little secret.

"This is my sister's, she likes to go all out and live a more leisurely lifestyle," I said with a remorseful smile, hoping that she didn't ask any more questions. Lies and truth. She used this vehicle just as much as I did.

"Oh my gosh. You really didn't need the money," Clover said, exasperated. She self-consciously looked over her attire and I grabbed her hand.

"You look beautiful," I complimented. I didn't want her self-conscious on this trip. Yes, I had money and I often forgot that sometimes people were uncomfortable by it, but I wanted to spoil her in this way. She seemed to ease back into the seat. Again, I could feel Allen's gaze watching us, bemused.

"Thank you. So, are you going to tell me where we're going?" she asked.

"No."

"How do I know you're not kidnapping me?" she tormented.

I gave her a wicked smile. "You don't."

The sexual tension immediately rose around us, and we both descended into silence. Desire lingered in an unspoken atmosphere of lust. Clover crossed her legs, as if as uncomfortable by the savage need as I.

After thirty long minutes of raw tension, we finally stopped moving. Allen opened Clover's door, revealing past the tinted windows the airport we'd arrived at. We were on a private strip, a jet waiting for us as we arrived on schedule.

Clover was powerless to hide her shock. "You have your own jet?" I found myself wrapped in male pride. From what I understood, Clover hadn't been able to go to many places and all she wanted to do was travel. I hoped that this trip would spoil her for inspiration once again and spark her passion for travel writing. I wanted at the very least to be able to do this for her.

"Consider it apart of the package I managed for us. A friend helped me organize this." Partially true. It was our family jet. In truth, it'd been over a year since I'd used it personally for a leisure trip. I could sense her hesitation as her bag was carried onto the jet.

"Please tell me where we're going," Clover asked.

"Trust me," I said, offering my hand out to her again. I wanted it to be a surprise and offer her a wow factor that no other male had given her. *I wanted to be remembered.* "I promise I'm not kidnapping you, although I make no promises against tying you up."

Her cheeks flushed red, and with reluctancy she grabbed my hand as I led her onto the jet. She looked over her shoulder, as if watching Allen drive away was her last opportunity to run, and I supposed to a degree it was.

"After you," I offered, guiding her to take the first step. Cautiously, she entered. White leather and wood trim decorated the warm cabin. She was in awe by its immaculate condition. I had to give credit where it was due; my father did have good taste.

I gestured toward the first set of reclining leather couches, opposite one another, a wood and golden-trimmed table between. A large-screen television positioned in perfect view of the chair she sat in. The small mini bar was already prepared at the back of the cabin with an assortment of beverages and food.

Clover seemed enthralled by the selection of magazines neatly arranged on the table between us, including the recent edition of *Candice*. Surprisingly though she gravitated toward *Be True*. It was the recent edition, including exclusive photos and interview with the famed ballerina, Sarah Hine.

"Do you read *Be True* magazine even though it's a rival magazine?" I asked as I settled in the seat across from her.

"Not as much as I used to," she admitted. "But I try to follow the work of one of their columnists. I'm envious of her writing." She flicked to the two-page spread and with a brief glance, I knew exactly who she was talking about.

"Oh? Who might that be?" I feigned ignorance.

"She goes by the name Anonymous."

"If they're called Anonymous, what makes you assume it's a woman?" I asked while grabbing a bottled water that was already sitting on my side table.

"Because there's a raw sensitivity in her voice. I've always just assumed it was a woman. I've been reading her work for years. There's something about her writing that I really resonate with. Do you find that weird?" She looked up at me, as if she'd be judged or exposed by her admission.

"I don't think that's strange at all." In fact, I found it endearing. Our gaze lingered as the seat belt sign lit up. This woman was almost insufferable. The moment I caught hold of those soft brown eyes, my gaze immediately dropped to those plump lips. Needing and wanting, it was a forever turbulent dance with Clover that tested my self-control. I slowly buckled my seatbelt, to strap myself, for more reasons than one.

Clover blushed red as she followed suit, quickly drawing her attention back to the page. She flicked through to the back of the magazine and flushed, as if trying to dispel the heavy tension. I grinned, finding great satisfaction in watching her squirm. She cleared her throat. "Would you like me to read your horoscope?"

"Do you believe in horoscopes?" I asked, still captivated by her. I was learning some more about her every day.

I noticed the bobble in her throat. "Not necessarily but I always enjoyed reading them with my sister." She seemed *very* preoccupied by the page.

"Why not. I'm a Scorpio."

Her grip went white knuckled on the page as she began reading. She seemed to squirm uncomfortably as she read out an embarrassing passage about temptation and an encounter with a new flame. She hastened through her own and we both read our respective magazines in silence, the thick heat of desire choking us both of words.

Neither of us attempted conversation over the next twenty minutes, and when I eventually gathered the courage to look at her again, she'd already fallen asleep. There was a subtle satisfaction in watching her sleep so easily within my presence. But more worrisome that she was so tired. It almost felt like a reflection of myself.

I wanted to help her. And in my own way, I hoped she felt liberated after this weekend getaway. I couldn't entirely understand my actions myself, but I was compelled to be the reason for her smiles and stealing a moment of that happiness for myself.—an unfamiliar notion that had me second-guessing myself every time I created an excuse to see her. I was selfishly stealing time, drawing this temptation out, and yet I couldn't simply walk away. Not yet.

Chapter 24

Clover

When I woke, Damon was staring at me contentedly with his elbow resting on the leather chair. He smiled at me as I roused. "Good morning, sunshine," he taunted. "You drooled."

Mortified, I wiped at my mouth and sat upright. To my surprise, wrapped around me was a blanket. "Did you put this on me?" I asked, noticing that the plane did feel cooler than when we first stepped in.

"You had goose bumps on your arms, so I assumed you were cold. I've been waiting for you to wake up. We landed about ten minutes ago."

"Why didn't you wake me?" I asked, looking through the peephole window.

"Actually, it's the cutest thing. Did you know you

talk in your sleep? You and I were having a fabulous conversation." He grinned. I felt the color drain from my face.

"What did I say?" Dread washed over me as his smile widened even further,his grin devilish.

"Well, let's just say the usually calm and collected Clover has no filter when she's having an imaginative dream..."

Heat spread across my cheeks again, with no memory of any dream. *Was he teasing me?* "Shouldn't we get going?" I asked, clearing my throat. I looked down at my silver wristwatch, which stated it was now 10:30 a.m. The flight had taken us three hours.

"After you," he said, gesturing toward the door. After collecting my handbag, we made our way to the door. I squinted, the bright sun offensive to the eyes. We were in a small clearing with trees, but I could make out a larger landing area for planes in the distance.

"Where are we?"

"Welcome to the Bahamas," Damon said casually. His chest brushed across my shoulders as he gently pushed past me and descended first. He turned and held his hand out, assisting me with the last few steps gentlemanly.

"We're in the Bahamas?" I evaluated my clothes and wished I'd worn shorts. The moment I'd stepped off the plane I was certain I was turning into a heated puddle and mess. Damon casually led me through customs, an effortless excursion as he held my hand guiding me through the entire process. *This felt like a fairy tale. The Bahamas?* My head was reeling with mixed emotions. It wasn't long until we'd cleared through the entry point, most of it a blur while I was still spinning from my sudden surprise.

A sleek black car picked us up and without direction, drove us to our accommodation. I stared outside the window in bewilderment, passing rows of Caribbean pine trees. It was a spectacular change from the hustle of Manhattan. Damon seemed smug as he watched me from his peripheral instead of the beautiful scenery outside. Anxiety and giddiness coiled in my stomach. *Who was this mysterious man beside me really?*

It wasn't long until we were driving along a pebbled driveway, leading to a pale-yellow, two-story villa with two large bay windows decorating the large front wooden door. There were two small balconies on the second floor, which I imagined to be attached to bedrooms. The ground was surrounded by rich foliage and a manicured freshly mowed lawn.

The moment I stepped out of the car, the smell of salt hit my nose. We must've been so close to the ocean. The driver took our bags and silently went ahead, guiding us through rows of more Caribbean pine trees to the front door.

"What do you think?" Damon asked, gesturing at the villa.

I was surprised. Most women would swoon over this but it made me feel even more conflicted. I wanted to embrace it, but I couldn't help but think why and why me? What was Damon getting out of this? But even if I asked he probably wouldn't answer. I didn't want to ruin the magic of it all either. I knew that this wouldn't last between us, so I decided to enjoy what I could now—my own Cinderella moment.

"Uncomfortable. I mean, I wore my jeans, long shirt, and everything."

His smile spread, seemingly relieved by my response. As out of my control as the situation was, I couldn't resist the sense of adventure he'd afforded me. I had always wanted to travel and was now presented with the perfect weekend getaway.

"Well then, let's get you into something comfier," he said with his hands still strapped to his pockets. "And then I'll show you the gardens."

"The gardens?" I echoed as we walked together toward the villa.

"There are some gardens nearby which are popular with locals and tourists. Who knows maybe it'll inspire you to write about it." He winked. An unsure smile spread over my face. Was he trying to encourage my writing?

The wooden two-door entrance was stunning. It led into a main room with a white marble floor and a magnificent glass chandelier overhead. It glimmered in the sunlight that crept through the windows. On my right was a room with white couches, an ornate coffee table, and an antique green vase with fresh vibrant yellow flowers. A half wall separated it from a spacious, modern kitchen with a blue marble counter and three bar stools arranged underneath it. An enormous, double-door stainless steel fridge hummed soothingly beside a small wine rack and, to my delight, an expensive-looking coffee machine.

When looking through the open wall, I could see the large window and floor-to-ceiling sliding doors. Outside, past the trees and in the distance, I could make out white sand and the green sea. Long white stairs led into a second level to explore.

Oh my. This wasn't a bed in breakfast or some

motel. He'd hired out the entire place. *Unless he owned it.*

"Your room's upstairs, Clover." Damon gestured, his hot breath brushing on the back of my neck. I was startled back to reality, flustering under his presence. Was Damon secretly some kind of millionaire?

"My room?" I asked skeptically.

"Your room. But I intend on visiting it both nights," he charmed as he wrapped his hands around my hip and kissed me on the cheek again. Just as quickly, he let go and motioned up the stairs, breaking the spell. He seemed almost childlike and excited to show me the second level. The entertainment room upstairs contained a pool table and a few white couches with a mini bar.

The two bedroom doors to my right were invitingly open. They looked like guest rooms when I compared them to the larger room on my left. With a glimpse, I took in an attached bathroom, walk-in wardrobe, and king-sized bed. Beside that room, a white marble bathroom with a spa was fitted with a mirror that lined an entire wall.

A breeze of salt air swept through, inviting me into the room to peer outside the window. My skin tingled as the air revitalized my pores. Damon left my bag beside the bed, watching me as I enjoyed the breeze. This was what I had always wanted—to explore somewhere new, and then to write about it. And it was Damon who helped me achieve it.

A small smile passed my lips as I brushed my hand over the smooth wood of the exquisite four-poster bed. *Isn't it funny how all of this has happened because I didn't sign that check,* I thought idly, looking at him. I held the post firmly, my nails edging into it as I reeled with desire for him. Suddenly the expansive space seemed hot and insufferable.

The breeze swept gently through my hair, startling me back to reality. "Thank you, Damon," I said. I tightened my grip on the solid bed frame, stopping myself from acting on the hunger that rose from my stomach and spread down my legs.

"Does that mean you're impressed?" he asked in a low voice.

I poked my tongue inside of my mouth, feeling flushed by his charm. *"Very,"* I huskily said as I confidently removed my shirt. Damon's eyes grew wide with hunger. "It means you left a slight impression, yes," I admitted breathlessly. The room was getting too hot again, and my legs began to feel heavy. I bent over, pulling my jeans down as well. "Consider this my way of thanking you. The gardens can wait."

Chapter 25

Clover

"I have a full day planned out for us," Damon announced boldly, intertwining his fingers with mine. My heart fumbled, still not entirely used to his touch and sentiment. I wondered if there was any way to get used to someone such as Damon and this fairy tale I seemed to have landed in. And in the back of my mind, all I could hear was the nagging reminder that this had to come crashing down to an end.

"But we only just arrived," I said, admiring the Garden of Groves. The garden was alive with lush foliage and glittering fountains.

"Don't you want to make the most of it and see as much as we can? The Bahamas is popular in tourism, perhaps you can write an article and submit it to another magazine."

I side-eyed him, finding the contrast of his deep maroon shirt and bright natural colors of the gardens almost humorous, and yet it seemed more to his personality. His sunglasses hung over his collar casually as we looked for a shadier spot.

"Are you trying to convince me to quit my job?" I asked skeptically. *Why did he care so much?*

"Not necessarily. I just think you deserve to be treated better and any magazine would be lucky to have you and your talent. It's just a suggestion," he said sheepishly. His grip tightened around mine, a response I wasn't even sure he was aware of.

Damon confused me, and I fought myself from wanting to delve in any deeper. He definitely wasn't who I thought he was. Was this *all* fake? Surely, there was some part of him, deep down that was being earnest. Surely, he was interested in me.

"Have you ever left a job that made you unhappy?" I asked curiously. I didn't expect much of an answer, but I hoped for it. As other couples walked around us, I wondered how they might see us. An ordinary couple or did we look mismatched on the surface? We stopped in front of a glistening waterfall. The gushing sound of it falling over rocks offering serenity.

"I considered quitting the family business once. I was caught in a scandal of sorts and it became pretty public. It drew a negative impact on my family and so I decided it was best if I stepped away entirely. But my sister wouldn't have a bar of it," he chucked to himself. "Instead, we agreed I'd lay low for a while, but it just hasn't felt the same since."

He led me over to a bench where we could watch fellow tourists and enjoy the ambiance of the bright day and splashing water. I couldn't help but feel like we were being watched and scanned our surroundings. Nothing but tourists. Great, and now I was becoming paranoid.

"What kind of scandal?" I asked. I knew I could only probe so much from him, but I didn't want to settle for the very little I knew about him. His answers only made him sound more elusive. I knew that this wouldn't be long term; I felt that wall and expiry date. My heart clenched at the very thought of when that might be. I didn't want to admit it, but I'd let this escort in. Somehow, he'd made an impression and it was making it harder to think about letting him go when he was never mine to begin with.

He was staring at his feet now, uncomfortable by the question. Innocently, he looked into my eyes. I expected him to close up like he usually did or wave it away with some charismatic charm, but instead he looked back to the waterfall, his demeanor changing to slight dejection.

"I had a girlfriend. She's part of a well-known family in New York. Her father runs a tech company. We'd been together for two years and then I found out she was pregnant."

I felt my stomach drop, the thought unsettling. Not at the thought of him being a father... but to think of him with another woman. I wanted to slap myself then for the thought. *Of course he'd been with other women.* And I'd been with other men, but the thought was still nerve wracking. How quickly was I falling for this man?

"I was surprised at first, but then ecstatic. Before we had the chance to tell anyone my best friend stepped forward and claimed that it wasn't my child but his instead. What a fucking whirlwind those next few months were."

He was still angry, I realised. "Was it yours?" I asked quietly, too scared that he'd pull away from me in consequence. His girlfriend and best friend cheated on him. Could you blame the guy for being on the defence? And yet that curdled my stomach thinking maybe he thought the same of me or every other woman he'd be with.

"No. I fired my best friend, and never saw either of them again."

I fought against prying further, respecting him and grateful for what he'd already shared. But I quietly added, "How long ago was that?"

As if snapping out of his simmering thoughts, he stared back at me again, a softness filling him instead. "Two years ago. But that's then and this is now," he, said gently raising my hand and kissing it. My heart stammered. But was there a difference? Was I just some rebound girl for him to waste his time with? And for whatever reason it was shattering to think I was just a distraction. But could I really deny that he was doing the same for me.

Again, I felt that looming sense that someone was watching. I turned and looked around, still only finding other couples and tourists walking or merrily having picnics.

"Clover?" he asked.

"Sorry, I just feel like we're being watched. I know that sounds crazy," I admitted. "But I'm sorry that happened to you. No one deserves that, but I hope it leads you to something better and it sounds like your sister really helped you out. She sounds amazing. My sister probably would've beaten the shit out of the other guy."

Damon threw his head back and laughed, his genuine humor swelling me with a warmth I didn't entirely understand. *What was this man doing to me?*

"If she could've I think Michelle would've as well."

"Hell hath no wrath like a sister's fury," I joked. He wiped away small tears from his eyes. I wondered how long it'd been since he'd laughed so boldly.

One of the groundskeepers walked up to us with a gentle smile. "Would you like me to take a photo?" they politely asked.

"Oh." I was almost shocked by the suggestion. We'd taken a photo together before at the masquerade ball. But this felt different. Our circumstances were different.

"Sure, thank you," Damon said offering his phone and put his hand around my waist. I leaned in, searching his eyes with uncertainty. Didn't we look like a couple? Was I starting to fall for my own game and lies?

"Clover you have to look at the camera," he said, not diverting his gaze from mine either.

Simultaneously, we looked away, bearing bright

charismatic smiles, switching on work mode. The polite groundskeeper gave us the thumbs-up and handed back the phone. It was two photos. One of us staring at one another, and if I'd been an outsider, I might've dared say it looked like we were... in love. The next was also a beautiful photo, the scenery stunning in the background, with nice smiles. But it said nothing of what was happening between us like the first. We were gravitating toward one another and in a potent way.

And with that very thought, Damon leaned in and kissed me, his tongue making a claim once again. And as usual, I melted into him, unable to resist.

Chapter 26

Clover

Shortly after, we found ourselves hand in hand walking toward a local restaurant, instead of talking about the heaviness of Damon's past. Our conversation had since changed to places we'd like to travel, favorite authors and film adaptions. I was grateful he opened up but was also unsettled by the thought that I was just something to pass his time. And even though I knew this is what we were, a small part of me was still hopeful that maybe it could be something more. And with that very endearment, I felt like I was setting myself up for hurt and disappointment.

The restaurant was built on a wooden pier over the green ocean. Wooden tables and chairs lined the dining hall and offered an electric atmosphere as holidaymakers laughed and drank together, side by side in exotic paradise. The large floor-length wooden doors were left open, letting a small salty breeze to sweep through from the glimmering ocean. On our left was an impressive wine rack beside a large fish tank containing a small shark, swimming around. Overhead, bronze fans swept, circulating air through the room.

"Just a table for two?" a beautiful waitress asked us. The shimmery gold of her eye shadow contrasted beautifully with the dark glow of her skin. I wondered what it'd be like to live a Caribbean lifestyle. To live locally and soak up the sun most days. From what I'd seen, the locals looked really happy.

"Yes, please," Damon replied, gesturing for me to go first as she escorted us to our table, right near the open windows. She placed the menus down so we could look through them. Quickly, I spotted what I wanted—Seafood, of course.

"Would you like an entrée?" Damon asked while looking over his menu. He looked surprised when I lowered my menu my choice already made.

"No, I'm happy with my main and a glass of red wine," I said politely.

"Wow, you've selected what you want already?"

he asked. "I've never seen a woman choose so quickly."

"What are you saying; you've brought many women to this place? And here I thought I was special," I teased.

"You seem to forget, Angel Puff, that I've escorted many women. And they all seem to take hours to decide on the same old salad," he taunted with a cocky smile.

At the mention of his job, a heavy feeling gripped my stomach. I wondered again why he did the escorting? He didn't need the money, it seemed, so did he just get a kick out of it? If so, there was every chance he would regularly extend his 'services.' "Well, I'm not a salad kind of girl," I said in defiance, feeling bitter at the thought of being compared to other women.

"No... no, you're definitely not," he agreed with a smile that quickly burned away my slight discomfort.

I looked out at the water, mesmerized by its beauty and considered a different lifestyle, imagined what it would be like to live here? This had always been the goal, hadn't it? To travel to exotic places and write about it. But in the two years of living in Manhattan, I hadn't gotten any closer.

The subtle click of a camera dispersed my

thoughts. I looked up at Damon, startled that he'd taken a photo of me while I was deep in thought. "Did you just take a photo of me?" I asked.

"I'll send that one to you too." He charmed a smile.

"I can't help but think you're starting to make a game of this photo taking thing," I cocked an eyebrow.

"Maybe I am."

"Challenge accepted." I smiled back, relieved to see the waitress coming back to take our order because I was starving.

I could feel my skin burning and turning into a darker shade of bronze under the sun's hot glow. As the sun soaked into my skin, I became more dehydrated with each sip of wine that passed by my lips. I couldn't so easily spark conversation with him. I wanted so much more. I couldn't fathom the pull; how and when did my body become so consumed by his gaze? When did our games take hold over my heart and body?

We finished the afternoon with a walk along the

beach and came across a hut that advertised sunset horse-riding tours. The sunset framed the ocean and bathed the island in a warm glow.

Joining another two families and a couple, Damon and I held back to admire the scenery and to take a few photos. The sun's glow over the water caught my eye as if reminding me that this really could be my full-time job. I also couldn't help but admire Damon's silhouette on horseback, the sunset casting his shadow on the white sand.

I laughed hysterically when he tried to pose in front of me as I held the camera. He leaned too far back at an angle the horse didn't appreciate, and it threw him off. He was uninjured, but I hadn't the time to ask him if he was all right before I erupted in uncontrollable laughter.

"You think that's funny, do you?" he asked, brushing himself off, then guiding his horse toward me by its lead. I couldn't hold it in, if only I'd gotten *that* on camera. "What if I threw you in the water, then? And leave you for the crabs," he suggested playfully, stomping over to me.

I raised my leg to him, pushing him back in hysterics. "No, my horse won't let you near me," I said, still kicking him away.

He managed to grab my leg, carefully to ensure

he didn't startle the horse. His hand remained while birds flocked overhead, grabbing our attention. It was all so stunning; I'd never experienced anything as beautiful. For the first time in a long time, I felt like I could breathe. We both looked on in awe of the beautiful Bahama waters and sun. I pulled out my phone, focusing the camera on the top of Damon's head while he was distracted.

"Damon," I whispered. As he turned to me, I clicked the photo, finally getting my first photo of him looking surprised. He'd stockpiled far too many of these throughout the day and I finally felt triumphant capturing such an innocent expression on him.

"You're sneaky," he said with a smile. I once again erupted in laughter when I looked at his horse, recalling him falling.

"It's not funny," he said, tapping my leg, trying to hide his smile. "I could've been seriously hurt, and then what? Would you have raced me to the villa on your horse?"

"Are you guys coming!" the instructor yelled back to us huffily.

I bit my bottom lip, trying to contain my laughter. "I guess you'll never know," I teased, lightly tapping my horse so she would catch up with the rest. He watched me from behind for a while. And when I looked over my shoulder at him with a smile, I nodded my head forward in a "C'mon!" gesture.

With a smile, he jumped back onto his horse, speedily coming to my side.

Chapter 27

Damon

The day had slipped right through our fingers like sand in an hourglass. Every moment spent with Clover seemed to escape me like we never had enough time and I found myself almost clutching at it, in disbelief that this weekend would soon come to an end. My body felt alive with Clover around and I was shocked even in myself for having opened up to her about Annabelle and Michael.

I stopped dead in my tracks as we arrived at the villa just after nightfall. Michelle was standing at the front door waving her hand around like a lunatic as she was on the phone. My stomach dropped.

"Who's that?" Clover asked curiously.

"My sister," I growled, all venom. *Why was she*

here? The moment she spotted our car, she ended the call and snapped it shut with hand on hip casually. Despite her laid-back attire with a bikini top and deep-purple sarong that wrapped around her hips that to most would scream "relaxed tourist," I knew better. Nothing got past my sister and it was her wandering nose in my affairs that led her here.

I steadfastly approached my sister, almost defensively so she couldn't crane her head around to assess Clover effectively.

"What are you doing here?" I growled.

"I could ask you the same. You could imagine my surprise when I found out about your little getaway trip with the jet and to our family villa."

"And so you decided to *stalk* me?"

She snorted. "Please I'm not a stalker here, and need I remind you about Benjamin Thomas, head of the football team, when you punched him in front of all my friends at high school for calling me something vulgar. And you weren't even invited to that party. That's stalkerish," she tsked me bitterly.

"Yea well he deserved it," I quipped. "And I was seventeen." The hormones might've been running at an all-time high then. But barging in on campus and an island holiday were two completely different extremes.

"I came here because I was worried about you," she finally admitted, somewhat defeated.

She craned her head around to look at Clover and raised an eyebrow. "And now I don't know what to make of this," she said quietly.

My heart stopped as if she was sizing Clover up. What was I meant to say? Clover was... it wasn't just like I'd brought a fling to the island... But she couldn't be anything more than that either. I felt unusually protective of whatever this was Clover and I shared. "Don't mention anything about the Brogardt family, please."

My sister raised her eyebrow. "Keeping secrets are we now, little brother? Having an identity crisis?"

But when I didn't find humor or reply to her jab she seemed to soften. She circled around me, all natural charisma and warmth on display. "Hi, I'm Michelle, Damon's long-suffering older sister."

Clover greeted her with a polite smile, although she was very much confused. "I'm Clover. It's lovely to meet you. I feel like I've seen you somewhere before."

My heart froze. Michelle casually waved her hand around. "Possibly in Manhattan? The city isn't as large as most might think." I cringed at the familiar phrase, I'd said the same thing when

Cassidy thought she'd recognized me. But Clover didn't dispute it.

Michelle continued, "This is so embarrassing. Our family friend lets us use this villa from time to time, but I didn't realize we booked it at the same time. Sorry." I closed my eyes, grateful that she wasn't outing me. All my libido had suddenly dropped with my sister here.

The door opened and Phillip poked his head outside. He adjusted his glasses and mouthed "sorry."

"Ah, and this is my husband, Phillip. Honey, this is Clover, Damon's, ah, friend. Come in, come in. Let's have some wine!" She seemed to skip back as he opened the door wide.

I grabbed Clover's hand. "I'm so sorry, I had no idea they would be here as well. We can find a hotel for the night."

"It's fine," she said with a small smile. "I'm surprised but the more the merrier right?"

Surprised was an understatement, this was a downright calculated ambush. I unnervingly felt on edge, like I didn't want Clover crossing over anymore into my world, terrified of what damage it may cause. Just like the last time. Not for my family but for her. She deserved better than this.

I broodily led Clover through the door. What kind of hell had this turned into? Michelle sprang back out, despite Phillip's obvious complaints. "Damon, you won't believe the collection Mr. Lanter has offered us from his wine shed beside the ocean. Apparently, the shed was meant to store his jet skis and things, but his ex-wife kept drinking them all, so he hid them there, but he's worried about what state they'll be left in if he leaves them too long. He encouraged us to help ourselves," she said animatedly, obviously already tipsy. "Come, Clover; let's partake in some wine tasting together."

She linked her arm through Clover's, dragging her away without hesitation. My arm was outstretched behind her, as if ready to fight over her with my sister like our childhood toys.

Phillip stepped outside, adjusting his glasses and making sure his wife was out of earshot. "I'm sorry. I told her we shouldn't pry. You know how she gets when she's worried. When we were alerted about the jet she was packed and in the car within thirty minutes."

I clenched my jaw. "She's crazy."

"I know," Phillip agreed. "Which is why I'm madly in love with her. But also, you've lived with her for longer remember?" He smiled. I'd always liked Phillip. Owning his own accountant firm, they were completely opposite in many ways but worked so well together. And to a degree, he really settled Michelle down. But unfortunately, that seemed to give her the luxury of meddling in other people's affairs, like my own.

She'd always been so full of life, even though she had dark circles under her eyes from her busy working schedule. And I could tell she was enjoying this beyond measure.

"I've been waiting all afternoon! I even organized a few cheese platters." She waved her hand around to swirl the wine before taking another sip and guided Clover through the sliding doors to a spacious garden area. Phillip offered me a beer, and I took it begrudgingly. This evening was now cemented in. How did my weekend getaway with Clover so easily become highjacked?

Outside to the right were two lounge beds and hammocks. They both opted for a lounge bed and settled back on the comfortable white cushions. She offered Clover a glass of red wine, encouraging her to drink. My sister also had a talent for being a bottom-less wench when it came to alcohol.

"Phillip, could you whip us up dinner? It's your night to cook," Michelle called in a sing-song voice.

He looked at her adoringly and agreed easily. I felt my jaw tighten, he was completely whipped, but in every action he adored her, worshiped her and would do anything for her. He leant over and kissed Michelle on the forehead before obediently leaving.

"Are you coming?" Phillip asked.

"You too, Damon," Michelle demanded, waving me off. She looked over her shoulder at me, relishing in my warning glare. "We're going to have some girl talk!"

"It's okay, Damon," Clover encouraged and my heart dropped. Unknowingly she was encouraging my sister's antics. And although I knew Michelle would do nothing to hurt me, I was jealous she was stealing what precious time I had left with Clover. And without doubt, I was nervous that she'd let something slip about who we truly were.

Chapter 28

Clover

Instead of heading into the kitchen, Phillip grabbed car keys and left, Damon trailing behind him like he'd just been scolded. "I wish it was so easy to command them to cook," Michelle laughed to herself. "I bet they've driven across the island to Phillip's favorite restaurant to pick something up." She took another sip of her wine approvingly.

Michelle was stunning and Damon's older sister in every way. She was beautiful, long-legged, long dark-brown curly hair, and with the same molten brown eyes and olive tan as Damon. She looked to be in her late thirties, and as she drew closer, I could appreciate the strong scent of her expensive perfume.

Her husband was no different; they both looked like they'd come out of a fashion magazine. However, in looks and personality, I had the sense that the two were very different. Phillip was fair-skinned, blonde-haired, and had blue eyes. He was equally as well-groomed, and I judged him to be in his forties.

"How long have you been married?" I asked, appreciating the red wine.

"Nine years, and it's been the best nine years of my life. Don't believe the rumors that marriage is all hard work," she said with a smile. "So tell me a little about yourself, Clover, and how'd you meet my brother?"

I choked on my wine.

"Are you okay?" Michelle asked finding the closest napkin. Embarrassed, I took it wiping at my mouth.

"Sorry it just went down the wrong way," I lied, gathering my wits. I couldn't tell her the truth. "At a work function."

"Oh really?" she asked, surprised. Shit, this probably wasn't good. "What kind of event?"

"I work for a magazine in New York, and we had a masquerade event. We met there."

"What magazine?" She asked, her gaze narrowing. As if quickly realizing my discomfort, she lightened. "Apologies, you have to excuse me. My brother's been rather distant lately so I'm not sure what he's been up to. I didn't realize he was seeing someone, so this has come as a surprise."

"Is that because of incident?" I blurted out the question before I even had time to think. *He said it happened two years ago. Maybe they didn't have friction because of it anymore.*

"The incident?" she asked politely.

I couldn't avoid it now since bringing it up. "With his ex and best friend?"

Her eyebrows shot up. "He told you about that, huh?" She absentmindedly topped my glass up again.

"Briefly, I didn't want to pry anymore than he'd told me."

Michelle seemed like a woman who often didn't give much away, most likely something her and her brother had in common. She finally sagged back into the chair comfortably again. "Annabelle and Michael ruined his life. She'd been one of my best friends as well which made it harder on everyone. But I guess you don't know someone until they show themselves. But it's been two years since then. He deserves to move on. I'm not surprised to hear Michael cheated on her and has moved onto the next woman already although Damon refuses to talk about it."

I flinched under this new piece of information. He hadn't mentioned that. But did it matter?

"My brother's a genius, and don't tell him I said that because I'll deny it. But he's always thrown himself into work and always looked after our family. But I worry that's all he has. That's why I was surprised to see you here, he hasn't taken any interest in a woman since Annabelle. But you... you've seemed to have piqued his interest."

I swallowed that. Could she mean that the feelings I was having for him were mutual? I wanted to believe it. Deep down I did, but I felt like there was a presence looming over us. Something I didn't entirely trust. Or maybe it was my paranoia because all my other relationships were short lived. Would he tire of me as I had done in the past with others?

"I just hope he finds what he's looking for," I said, doubt clouding me once again.

"And you don't think that could be you?" she carefully asked.

I dropped my gaze, confronted by her question. Even if I wanted it to be me...

"Sorry, that was rude. Phillip often tells me I'm too direct." She smiled. "And besides we were talking about you anyway, what role do you work at your magazine?"

I was grateful for the change in subject, plucking an olive off the cheese platter board. "I'm a personal assistant to Debra Coorman at *Candice Magazine*."

"Really?" she drawled out with piqued interest. "I've heard she's quite the force to be reckoned with."

"You're familiar with the publishing industry?" I asked.

She hesitated, as if choosing her words carefully. "Somewhat. It always helps to know who's doing what in New York. You seem like the type who wants more than simply being someone's assistant though?"

She sounded so similar to her brother that it was uncanny. Both seemed like very driven individuals and career orientated. But I supposed that came with running their own family business, whatever it was. "I do. Ever since I left Ithaca my goal has to become a travel columnist. Unfortunately, it's been a hurdle to get there."

"You haven't pitched in-house or freelanced work?" she asked.

I felt almost embarrassed to be discussing it with her. As if I hadn't tried different ways or attempted to go in-house. But I didn't want to admit my own failings as well and the temperament of Debra. It would only sound like an excuse. "I've done a few freelance pieces. The work pile built up very quickly though. I hardly have time for myself let alone pitching elsewhere at the moment. I suppose at some point I forgot about it. I have Damon to thank for that actually, he reopened my eyes to focus on what was important again. I guess sometimes we all need a bit of a shake-up. I suppose I'd found myself in a rut without realizing it." I smiled sadly to myself. "I'm sorry I'm blabbering."

"No," Michelle said reclining back into her seat more comfortably. "We've all been there. Maybe you and Damon have helped one another more than you realize." She offered the small cheese platter again. "Cheese?"

It was easy to settle into conversation with Michelle, her tension noticeably easing with every swig of wine. And the woman had an eye for when the glass was near empty. She kept filling us up, leaving no time to waste. We were giggling away in no time and opted to try the hammocks, easing back in the delightfully warm breeze.

Damon and Phillip waltzed through the doors with a few hot food platters in hand. Michelle had been right; they did go to Phillip's favorite restaurant.

"Ah, just in time," Michelle said, swallowing the last of her wine. "We just ran out. Damon, can you grab some more wine from the shedy thing near the beach?"

"Don't you think you've had enough to drink already?" Damon asked as he placed his platter on the table.

"Don't backchat like that to your older sister," she pretended to scold. "Clover is out as well." I looked down at the few mouthfuls remaining in the glass. She gave me a glance that suggested I drink it, and quickly too. Under her watchful gaze, I downed it with a grimace and presented the empty glass in front of everyone like some party trick. The bitter red wine tasted stale in my mouth.

"Fine, what are you after?" Damon relented, placing his hands in his pockets.

"I don't know. Clover, I chose the last two bottles, can you go down and choose something nice for us?" she asked with a sly smile. Damon and I looked at one another, fully aware of how obvious his sister was.

Her directness amused me. Much like Damon, she liked to play her harmless games. Damon waited for me as I struggled to get out of the hammock. *This hammock is like a trap,* I thought to myself, trying to twist out of it.

I allowed myself a small smile in triumph when I succeeded. I walked over to him, trying to keep my steps steady. When we were no longer in hearing distance of Michelle and Phillip, he commented on my walking.

"Are you staggering?" he playfully teased.

"I am not." I slapped his arm, tripping over a branch and losing my footing. He caught me, and I held my breath, startled by my near fall. "I can't see a thing out here!" I growled, as if *that* was the reason I tripped over my own feet. His strong arms helped me stand, his touch creating a wildfire down my body.

The moonlight shimmered against his dark-brown, molten eyes. I resisted the urge to brush my hand along his stubble, so curious about this man. He'd once been so hurt, and when I looked into his eyes, I could only imagine that suffering. And it pained me to envision him going through that.

"Sure," he said in a sarcastic tone. A smile pulled at his lips as he straightened me onto my unsteady legs. In heavy silence, we continued walking toward the beach. Like Michelle said, it wasn't too far from the sea, and we could hear the rolling waves. A glimmer of the dark waves were highlighted by the moonlight.

A small wooden shack came into view. Damon fumbled with the key to unlock the door in the darkness before revealing the dark space beyond. We walked into the elaborate temperature-controlled room and pulled on the small hanging string, which filled the room with light. Mr. Lanter, who I later found out owned the home and was a client of Michelle's, had definitely gone to extremes to hide his stash. The light was swinging gently as the breeze crept in, creating moving shadows. The light highlighted neglected dusty shelves. I couldn't help but find amusement in the whole situation when I thought of the older wooden shack compared to Mr. Lanter's villa. No wonder his ex-wife never found the wine. I doubted she would have ever come to such a place if she was used to the splendor of the villa. On our right was a large rack of exquisite wines. On the left was a dirty old bench that could have once belonged to a handcrafter.

The air was still, and for a moment we stood in the semidarkness, waiting for our eyes to adjust while listening to the sound of crashing waves in the distance. Together, we looked over a few of the labels.

"So, what were you and my sister talking about?" he asked casually, placing one of the wine bottles back into the rack with disinterest.

"Just girl talk." I smiled lightly. "What was that one?" I asked, reaching out for the bottle he'd just put back. I stood closer to him to read over the label.

"This is a good one," I said, looking over my shoulder and up at him. He was staring at the thin strap of my silky white dress that had slipped down my shoulder. His eyes consumed me with hunger like they always did.

My mind told me in so many ways not to do it. I should know better, I had to slow this pace or only I'd be hurt in the process. But my body held a thirst that would not be quenched until I kissed him, touched him and claimed him all over again.

I moved slowly, brushing my lips against his, lapping in the warmth of his breath and inhaling it as my own. I brushed my bottom lip against his top one, encouraging him to take the lead. His hand slowly rose to my cheek, cupping it. I could see by the shimmer of his dark-brown eyes that he was tentative, as if holding back for the very same reason I was. With his sister here, reality was creeping in. This wasn't just our little secret anymore. And it could have damaging consequences. I brushed my fingers gently along his collarbone and wrapped my hand behind his neck to pull him closer.

The tension built as we gave in to the chemistry that pulsed through us. His lips pressed onto mine, spreading a fire through my body. I tightened my grip on the back of his neck, pulling him into me. I barely noticed my grip loosening and the bottle slipping onto a pile of wetsuits.

He twisted and pushed me against the wine rack. His kiss was like no other as he slowly created a flame I couldn't put out. It made my legs quiver as his arms pulled me closer to him, Damon's hands exploring my body. I pushed my hands through his hair, biting his lip. He pulled away and I opened my eyes, conscious of the sensation that quivered throughout my body. My nipples were hard, and a low rolling wave quivered up my legs, thumping heavily at my core.

After a brief hesitation, as if unsure of himself and coming to some kind of decision, he slammed me harder against the wine rack before collecting my lips again with his. His hand brushed along my shoulder and swept off one of my silky straps. I held firmly onto his belt, trying to rip away the buckle that was now my greatest enemy. His hands wrapped around my ass as he lifted and wrapped my legs

around his waist. He began to kiss down my neck-
Every kiss lingering like a searing flame.

Only the material of our clothing came between
what we both ached for. He lowered me onto the
bench; everything beyond him seeming like a blur to
my heightened senses. As he moved, each jolt only
stirred my need further. I could feel his length rising
near my inner thigh.

As he bent over me, I ran my hands along his
shirt buttons, desperate to feel his body against mine.
His naked chest was perfectly chiseled. The random
image and thought of him boxing, hot and sweaty
came to mind. There was a small amount of hair that
trailed further down past his belt. I kissed his chest,
loving the taste of his salty skin and the smell of his
cologne lingering in my nose. I continued to kiss
down, my lips brushing over the chiseled abs of his
stomach, claiming every inch as mine.

He pushed me back so I was lying flat and then
lowered himself over me. I savagely ripped at his belt
as he kissed me. One hand on the bench above my
head supported his body as he used the other to
gently move my hands away. I froze as he ran his
hand up my inner thigh. The silky material lifted as
he ran his hand underneath my dress and his thumb
brushed past the lining of my underwear.

He gently kissed over my collarbone and down toward my breasts, his hand simultaneously caressing me under the dress. The cool breeze swept over my hot skin as his other hand pulled my dress down over my purple silk bra. His fingers traced over my bra straps as he continued kissing down my chest. A moan crept past my lips as his fingers began to work my heated demand.

I could feel his now very hard shaft, which had me itching to grab it as I propped myself on my elbows, kissing him again.

He'd undone the belt I'd so horribly failed at taking off, freeing his hard shaft. I gulped audibly, the effects of the wine leaving my mouth dry and his cock looking like the only thing to give me salvation. "I want you, Damon," I said.

"I don't have a condom," he growled.

"Then we can find other ways to have fun," I said, leaning up and fisting his cock. He cupped my face again kissing me without excuse or reservation.

"I want you too," he admitted through heated breaths as he pushed away my hair that began to tangle in a sweaty mess. I tightened my grip at the base of his shaft, devouring the image of him reacting to how I played with him. "I just can't seem to stay away from you," he growled. His thumb rubbed over my clit, creating a shake through my entire lower body.

"Then don't."

In a broken shack with the glimmer of the moonlight shining through, we devoured one another like teenagers. Unapologetic for this heated thirst and hunger that we needed to fill.

Chapter 29

Clover

The fresh salty air drifted into our room, rustling the sheer curtains. My eyes fluttered open after what felt like the best sleep I'd had in years. I looked over to Damon, the reason for that, as I was delicately wrapped in his arms and chest. I shifted slowly, afraid to wake him. Embarrassingly, I watched him as he slept, his body freshly tanned from yesterday.

What was I going to do with him? Not being caught up in his charisma was difficult. Falling for him... Well I imagined that would be hard for any woman to resist. And I was shamefully discovering that I was not excluded from that.

My cell vibrated on the side table. Peering over, I was startled by the four missed calls. I sat upright, still trying my best not to stir Damon awake. *Why had Cassidy tried to call four times?* She was house-sitting for me, had something happened to Pudding?

I opened up the text and my eyes widened and my mouth went agape. There was a screenshot of Damon and me in the gardens yesterday. But that wasn't the most disturbing part of the article. The headline read: *'Has Billionaire Bachelor, Damon Brogardt moved on?'*

I clicked on the link and scrolled through the article, my mind turning into a chaotic whirlwind. *Billionaire bachelor?* Tears pinpricked my eyes as I read every word like a personal slap. How had I been so blind? And then it dawned on me why I'd recognised Michelle. *They were the CEOs of* Be True *Magazine. Damon was... I knew he was more than an escort... but this?*

"Good morning, beautiful," Damon said sleepily as he lazily stretched out and laid his hand on my leg. I was shell-shocked. He immediately sat upright. "What's wrong?"

Without words, I showed him the screen. His entire demeanor changed and with a clenched jaw, all he could manage to say was "I'm sorry."

"You're sorry?!" I erupted, surprised by my own

anger. I flicked his hand off, clambering out of the bed. I wanted to be anywhere but here.

"Clover, please." His hard chest rose and fell quickly. Panic spread across his face as he tried to explain himself.

I didn't want to hear it, no more. No more of this hurt. How many other things had he lied to me about? And yet I'd chosen to be ignorant about it all along, so why did the shock of it still hurt like this?

"I knew there was mystery behind the whole escort thing but this..." I pointed to my screen. "This is a joke! Do you have any idea what trouble this could cause me? I could lose my job!" Suddenly it dawned on me as to why he only attended masquerades and always wore shaded glasses. This was what he considered keeping out of the public eye? *But we fell for it.* Not even Debra caught on to his identity. How stupid I must've looked.

"Your job?" He seemed offended now. "Is that all you care about in all of this?"

I raised an eyebrow, hand on hip. "Are you kidding me? You think that my self-preservation is laughable when you've humiliated me to this degree! You lied to me, Damon! I *knew* this was too good to be true. I knew it would all fall apart. But it still fucking hurts so much!"

He went to say something but closed his mouth, an excruciating pain twisting his features. "I wanted to tell you, but you weren't like the others, you didn't treat me differently because of who I was or—"

I cut him off, pure rage bubbling over. "So you enjoyed the novelty of my companionship? Like some poor girl, rich guy experiment?" I began packing my bag.

"Clover, please it wasn't like that."

I couldn't see straight, think straight. "And yet you took me to the fucking Bahamas, couldn't restrain splashing a little cash, huh?"

He was angry now. "I'm not just some rich kid like you're making me out to sound like. I did this because I wanted to do it for *you*. Clover, everything I've done with you has been genuine. I swear to you that much. Everything I've felt—"

"Felt?" My voice wavered, a constriction forming around my throat. I knew it'd hurt. I knew this would end. *But why was it hurting so damn much?* I wanted to run, run away as far as I could from this place. From him.

"I don't even know who you are. Or more specifically, now I do and that's a *big* problem." Tears streaked down my face, his pained expression only cementing the knots in my stomach. I should've

Kia Carrington-Russell

known better. *Live a little,* I'd thought, and now I just wanted to laugh at myself. I had no one to blame but myself.

With a fury, I grabbed the last of my things—what I could see anyway. I just needed to get out of here.

"Clover, please just listen to me for a second." Damon tried to step in front of me, but I pushed him to the side, trying my damn hardest to keep it all together. I raised my chin, dignified as best as I could be in this situation.

"I hope you find whatever it is you're looking for Damon." I barged past him and out the door. I jumped over every second step down the staircase.

"Good morning," Michelle chimed with a frypan in hand. "I'm making—Clover?"

"Thank you for everything. It was lovely meeting you," I managed to say as I beelined for the door.

"Clover!" Damon called out, and before I knew it, my legs were carrying me barefoot down the driveway. I needed to be as far away from them as possible. Away from Damon. And away from this heavy broken feeling in my chest. I thought it'd be impossible to fall for him so quickly. And yet here I was with a pain I'd never felt before, not since my father's passing. And all I wanted to do was curl in a ball and cry for being so stupid. Why did I choose to let my walls down and be vulnerable with someone who couldn't even give me his real name? Why had I let him be the exception? I had no one to blame but myself.

Chapter 30

Damon

"Damon, what happened?" Michelle snapped for answers as Clover ran out the door. I wanted to give chase, but what right did I have? She literally ran away from me. What could I possibly say to make this better, to excuse what I'd done to her?

By the time I'd started to realize my feelings, it was already too late. I'd been too scared to tell her who I was, certain it was for her best interest. But I realized now how selfish it was; I was just keeping myself safe while she put herself on the line. I'd caused more carnage than I ever wanted to admit.

"Damon?" Michelle snapped me back into the oversized villa. It felt so empty now. Shame flooded through me. What did I think would happen between us? Had I been living in my own fantasy world as well?

I glumly admitted, "A photographer snapped a photo of us yesterday and she saw an article about it this morning."

Michelle seemed confused until she realized the insinuation. "Why did you lie to her about who you were?"

My mind scrambled. Every fiber of my being wanted to drag her back to this villa so I could try to explain. *But explain what exactly?* As if reading my thoughts, like she often did, Michelle placed her hand on my arm. "Not now. You need to give her some time."

I crumbled into myself, surprised by my own disarray. I wanted Clover back, content in my arms. But did I even deserve that chance with her? All I could imagine was Clover's disgusted expression with tears sliding down her face. How could I do that to her? What right did I have to even explain myself?

"You really like her, don't you?" Michelle said, crouching to my level. I hung my head in shame.

"More than I realized," I said, rubbing my face.

"Damon, why did you lie?"

I looked up at my sister, grateful that Phillip wasn't here to see me like this. This reminded me of those two years ago, and Michelle had looked at me in a similar way. *When she pitied me.* Michelle had always been there for me and over all these years, I paid my respects by pushing her further away. No wonder she suspected I was up to something coming here. Back then, I felt so humiliated, hurt and betrayed. But this time it was all *my* fault.

"I took a job and escorted her to a *Candice* masquerade ball. I've never told anyone my identity, that was our rule."

She dipped her head to the side, no judgement. "I thought you'd stopped the escorting."

"I did, but... I don't know how to explain, I just had the pull to accept this one. Everything happened so quickly afterwards. And before I knew it I was finding ways to spend more time with her. And now, I guess that time's struck out. I didn't want to lie to her, but then when it shifted from a job to something more... I couldn't tell her."

"You can only live in make-believe for so long, Damon," she urged gently.

"I know. I got caught up and I couldn't see straight."

"Love blinds us in a funny way."

Love? "It can't be love, we hardly know each other," I rationalized.

"If you were simply infatuated, my dear brother, you wouldn't be dishevelled on the floor after she left. There's no timeframe on love and it comes in many ways. Give her time. You're a Brogardt. You know what you want, and you make it yours every time."

I looked into the depths of my sister's eyes, who often reminded me of my mother. Her proud cheekbones and poised posture were always a resemblance of strength.

"But what if the damage is already done?" I asked quietly, surprising myself and almost scared of her reply. I don't think I'd ever had so much weight and self-loathing pin me down that I wanted to curl into a ball, and yet I felt like a child—forgotten and alone.

"You rebuild, Damon. Like we've always done." She patted me on the shoulder. "I'm going to organize the jet." I stood clutching at the side of the kitchen bench until my knuckles were white. I'd fucked up and I'd lost the woman who was the first breath of fresh air I had felt in years.

When Allen collected me from the airport, he said very little and made no inquiry as to why I was alone. Although I imagined the tension was enough to ensure anyone stayed away. I kept my shaded glasses on, ignoring anyone in my path and hoping none were photographers. An article or two was nothing but if it blew out of proportion like it did two years ago... It could be a disaster for Clover and her job. I'd royally fucked up.

"Sir?" Allen said, ripping me away from my thoughts. As we pulled up to my apartment building, I felt the revival of my inner demons and anger. Standing out the front, bundled in her coats was Annabelle. "Would you like me to have her escorted off site?"

"No," I glowered. After two years why'd she decide to show her face now? We'd promised we'd never see one another again, and yet here she was.

"Very well. I'll take your bags to the penthouse, then."

I stepped out of the car, the cool breeze doing nothing to affect my simmering temperature.

"Damon?" Annabelle stepped closer. "Wow it's been so long."

"You shouldn't be here." I glowered. She looked no different to two years ago. Maybe her hair was slightly shorter and slight bags under her eyes but I supposed that's what having a child would do to some.

"I know we promised... but. Well, a girlfriend sent me an article and then I found myself here."

I tried to restrain my face crinkling further in anger. I was furious with myself and wouldn't take it out on her, despite what she'd done to me those years ago.

"How's Michael?" I spat, reminding her of the choice she'd made. And it only infuriated me more that just because she saw a photo of me and Clover, she felt obliged to come here. I was protective of Clover, wanting to block her from the scrutiny of my world.

Annabelle couldn't meet my gaze, rugging herself up further. She offered a lopsided smile. "You know, you might find it ironic considering what I'd done to you. But Michael left me for one of my friends a few months ago." She chuckled to herself, ill-humored by the irony. "He only visits little Emily once a week now as if we meant nothing."

"If you thought you'd get comfort from me, you're sadly mistaken." I once would've given her the world. Now, I didn't have the time or patience. We'd closed that door a long time ago. And now I felt...

nothing but pity for her. All that anger and resentment I'd been holding onto, was suddenly gone. "Why are you here, Annabelle?"

She seemed to find something comical. "I know it's stupid. But when I saw that picture of you and that woman, a lot of emotions came up. I know I was in the wrong and I'm not asking for a second chance. But when it all happened, it just happened so quickly, and I felt like I'd never really been given the chance to apologize to you. When there was so much media around and scandal tracking our steps, I tried to hide away for most of it. But then you didn't reply to any of my calls and messages. And in a way I feel like I deserved what I've got now. But I wanted to say, even now two years later that I'm sorry. I'm not sorry for having Emily. But it really was only one night with Michael before then—"

"One night is all it takes."

"I know that. I'm not asking for your forgiveness because I don't think you'll ever give it to me. But it just felt right to come and see you and tell you I wish the best for you. I'm kind of relieved to see that you've moved on, if anything at all."

It felt like she'd slapped me in the face and it only infuriated me further that she still had such a hold over me, until realizing that it wasn't because of her at all. All those feelings of resentment I'd been harboring for so long were suddenly gone; only to be replaced by a bitter pain of letting Clover slip through my fingers. Without realizing it, the time I'd spent with her had changed me. I had no reason to hold onto the hurt of the past anymore. Because now I had to focus my everything into begging Clover's forgiveness. Annabelle was right about one thing. I had moved on... even before I realized it.

"That's all I had to say," Annabelle added with a nervous smile. "And I know Michael will never apologize to your face. But I know he's sorry too. He loved you like a brother."

My hands felt clammy as I tightened them into fists, the mere mention of him sharpening an old hurt. *Because we had been like brothers.* Perhaps Annabelle I could quietly forgive, but Michael was an entirely different matter. "Apologizing for him even until the very end, huh?" I said, conflicted by the emotions erupting and overlapping one another. Was it time to let all of this go?

She shyly smiled again, a tear sliding down her face. "You can't help who you fall in love with right, even if you know it's not good for you. But I loved you too, Damon, and I hope you have the love and support you deserve."

She wavered down a cab. "Oh, how's Michelle doing?" she asked before opening the door.

I felt my jaw tighten. I didn't want her knowing or having anything to do with my family. She'd lost that right. As if realizing she'd overstepped, she dropped her gaze to the ground.

"Of course, sorry. Can you let her know, I said I'm sorry? I feel kind of relieved being able to say all these things to you tonight. So, thank you for listening and I won't bother you again."

She dropped into the cab and I watched her drive away, my heart hammering. I hadn't seen her for two years. And it was a mockery that she felt relieved by crawling back into my life and vanishing just as quickly. And yet I couldn't help but realize all of this—all of these emotions, of holding myself back with Clover—was somehow intertwined.

I was horrified to realize I was only hiding behind a mask as the escort, so that at any moment I could run. If it felt too real, I had an escape plan. And instead, she'd done the smart thing and ran from me.

"Sir, your luggage is in the penthouse. Have a good night," Allen said, stealing me away from my thoughts again.

I was a fucking mess.

Chapter 31

Clover

"I'd really appreciate if I could have this week off," I propositioned Debra. We were the only two in her office this early on a Monday morning. I'd hardly slept since the Bahamas and felt like I was going to fall apart any minute, and yet there was a sound resolve in me. I had every intention of going back to Ithaca for a few days. I just needed to be back home and process. I needed to get my things back into order.

The moment I returned to my apartment and saw Cassidy, I broke down and cried. Dark circles still rimmed under my eyes and I felt bone tired. It's as if all these years of little sleep and working long hours finally caught up on me and I'd just had enough.

"On such short notice?" she quipped. "Should we first discuss your conflict of interest relationship that'd I'd only recently been made aware of?"

She reprimanded me like a child in the principal's office. With as little information as possible I simply stated, "It won't be a problem anymore. We're over."

"Do you have any idea the amount of intel he could've discovered about us? You let our competition saddle right up in our very offices. Not forgetting to mention what you might've said in private. I can have you on instant dismissal."

"Then do it," I said coldly. Enough was enough. "Debra, I wasn't aware of Damon's position or the company he worked for. I'm also so sick and tired of your patronizing games. I'm a hard worker and I do everything I can for you and this company. And I don't know why you hate me so much but I'm so so tired. Aren't you?"

She seemed shocked by my confession. I continued. "You've stopped my growth at every step within your power. And right now, I'm asking you to please let me have a break. I'm only human and I'm so tired. Either you let me have a week off or I lodge every single issue and encounter of your bullying to HR. Whether it costs me my job, I don't care anymore.

"I'm leaving. And either I have a job to come back to or you have a court case on your hands. And I hope you choose the more peaceful way."

"Are you threatening me?" Her eyes narrowed and I no longer felt fear or constricted by my obligation and job. I felt nothing. And I didn't have the energy to put up with her shit anymore. Not right now. And despite her enjoyment of tormenting me, I did a lot of her work. Everyone was replaceable but I wondered if she had the time to spare to retrain someone new. It was a gamble I was willing to make *Had to make.* Because I *needed* this.

"I don't want to, Debra. I just want a break. A week, that's all I ask." I slapped a folder on her desk. "That's where I'm up to for the coming projects. Almost everything is complete. I can catch up on the rest next week when I come back."

She stood up, her face tormented and twisted in rage. "How dare you!"

But I ignored her, grabbing my handbag as I walked out, a weight sliding off me. It was a gamble. I could lose my job. But at this point, I really didn't care. Everything I'd worked so hard for, for what?

I hired the first car available to Ithaca, grateful to Cassidy for being able to look after Pudding a while longer. It'd been so long since I'd seen my family. How much had my nephews grown? I'd seen photos of Ethan and Christian when Megan sent them through text, but it wasn't the same as holding them in my arms and embracing my nephews or measuring their height against my own.

It was just a reminder of how many years had slipped by. In those two years I'd moved away, I'd only been back a handful of times. I was older now and almost missed that spark of youth that lacked in everyday responsibilities and ambition. I felt nostalgic thinking about what my once freer lifestyle had been. Now, only ambition consumed me. Until Damon came, I'd forgotten what the word "play" even meant.

I pushed any thought of him away, studying the town as I drove through it reminiscing. I thought Manhattan would be everything and now I was coming back depleted, like I'd been spat out. And my sudden decision to return home wasn't greeted with the excitement expected by my sister and mother. Instead, it was nothing but concern over the phone. I'd explained it then to Megan. All of it, how I'd met Damon and what happened at the Bahamas. But by then, I was all cried out, cold and clinical as I went through our short-lived timeline.

The small rosebushes that inhabited the front lawn had expanded, and the small pebbles leading up the driveway had darkened over time. It was a modest-sized home, one that suited my mother, sister, and two nephews perfectly.

Getting out of the car, I looked up at the screen door that was already opening. Megan and her two sons, Ethan and Christian, burst from the house and ran for me. I dropped to my knees as the boys ambushed me. One nephew on either side, I gave them a big hug, a wash of relief coming over me. *This is exactly what I needed. Home.* I was used to their smaller size and chubbier faces. I'd obviously missed out on witnessing a few growth spurts firsthand. I embraced their warmth, saddened I was missing so much of their growing up.

"I missed you, rugrats," I said, standing back up and opening my arms wide for my sister, who looked as beautiful and fit as ever.

"You took your time," Megan said with a smile, giving me a warm, welcoming hug. Over Megan's shoulder, I noticed Mom making her way out as her pet corgi, Jupiter, followed. Its legs were so stumpy it looked like at any moment it would trip, its ears flapping as the boys began to chase it around the front yard.

"What are you all going on about now?" My mother smiled, her green eyes pooling with warmth. My sunshine of a mother, that just looking at her filled me with such love and joy.

"Hello, Mamma," I said, embracing her tiny frame. Although her body had slightly aged, she still looked amazing for almost fifty-two.

"Welcome home, Clover," my mother said lovingly into my ear, giving me a kiss on the cheek.

"I'll help you with your bags," Ethan offered.

"No me!" Christian demanded as they had begun tug-a-war with the rolling travel bag.

"Boys! You can hold one side each!" Megan instructed. They both sagged in defeat and begrudgingly held either side and carried it together.

"Quick, I just put the kettle on," my mother instructed, wrapping herself in the warmth of her cardigan.

Megan kicked back behind, watching the others and offering me a worried glance. "Are you okay?" she whispered, too low for my mother to hear.

"Far from it," I replied honestly. "But I'll be better after Mom's homemade cookies I think."

Megan offered me a weak smile, not pressing any further.

The two-story home reminded me of a modern cottage. And in some spots, was noticeably outdated. There was now a brown stain on the white carpet in the hall. When I questioned where it had come from, Megan gave me a warning glare. Apparently, Christian had "accidentally" created that, and they couldn't get it out. My mother still grouched about it in the distance with light laughter that didn't entirely reach her eyes.

I walked through the lounge room to follow them into the kitchen. On the right side of the stairs were an office, laundry room, and the boy's room—which they shared.

Mom led me through the kitchen and into the backyard to show me her new rosebushes and began watering them as Megan carried the first glasses of wine out. *Midday drinking it was.* After a few more glasses, we were in hysterics. The time flew by ridiculously fast as I caught up on all the local gossip. And it felt like all my troubles in the world fluttered away. *Home.* This is what I'd been craving.

Later, I stumbled to the double bed in the guest room, embarrassed by my low tolerance of alcohol. I thought I'd have done better considering the amount I used to drink in the very same small town university. It made me consider contacting my old university buddy and best friend, Hayden. But the thought of leaving this house, in truth, felt like too much effort. Despite all my laughter during the day, the moment I was alone it all crept back in. The sadness and loneliness. The hurt and disappointment. And I only had myself to blame for it. I was usually so cautious and now I remembered why.

A light slap on the cheek jolted me awake.

Startled, and now very awake, I grimaced as Ethan and Christian jumped on me in excitement.

"Yea, get her. Show no mercy," Megan said, grinning as she leant against the doorframe. Although she was smiling, I noticed the aspirin and glass of water she was clutching onto desperately. Glad I wasn't the only one who woke up with a pounding headache and hangover. She tightened her aqua bathrobe, her blonde hair loosely spilling over her shoulders. "All right you two, go help Grandma make some toast," Megan said, ushering them away. With a disappointed moan and a quick kiss on my cheek, they both fled the room and scene of the crime.

"Here." Megan offered the glass of water and aspirin. "No rest for the wicked. Drink this so you're useful," she added with a vicious smile.

"You look like you're in worst shape than me," I murmured, pushing aside my tangled web of hair and downing the aspirin and water. "How's Mom?"

"Bouncing off the walls, cooking, the usual. To this day I'm still surprised that woman isn't an alcoholic. Neither of us can drink her under the table. Her tolerance is unbeatable," she said with a smile.

"Isn't that the truth? And also, she had to raise us, she had years of practice." I laughed.

"C'mon, stop stalling and get out of bed," she demanded, snatching her glass of water back and walking out of my room. Rubbing my eyes, I glumly followed.

I navigated the staircase clumsily and clutched the handrails for dear life. The light coming in from the front bay windows irritated my sensitive eyes. Perhaps I'd drunk waaay too much, but was as expected when catching up with my sister and mom.

I tightened my black cardigan around my sleeveless top paired with sweatpants, yawning. I could only imagine the state my hair would be in. After a stifled yawn, the enticing smell of coffee, bacon, and eggs in the kitchen wafted around me. My mother was busily humming away at the stove as she joyfully cooked. Megan poured juice for the boys, who sat patiently at the wooden table.

"Hurry, Clover, come and get it before it's all gone, these boys will demolish everything by the time you've sat down," my mother chastised. She was smiling as she served strips of bacon onto the plates. I poured the hot coffee into three mugs, passing one each to Megan and Mom, and then taking a cup for myself, smiling. I missed this.

The coffee went down well but waking up properly needed a larger nudge than that, and so my first hour of movement was done begrudgingly. After breakfast, Megan— not so sweetly—bossed everyone around, preparing them for school. Mom opted to take the boys to school and so Megan and I sat out in the backyard, bathing in the natural sunlight, sunglasses hanging over our noses.

"Here I snagged some of Mom's freshly baked cookies," she said, placing down a plate. Although I was full and possibly had mixed feelings about the food in my stomach right now, I still picked one up. Nothing beat Mom's homemade cookies.

"It's nice to be back," I admitted, examining the

cookie before taking a pleased bite. It just felt so much simpler here, without the hustle of the city. Without its interrogated complications and second-guessing my worth and ability at work.

Megan leaned back in her wooden, high-back chair. "It's nice to have you back. But you know you can't stay here forever."

I sighed, setting the cookie back down only one bite in. She'd been kind enough to not ask questions yesterday. But I knew she'd be itching to know. I'd told her everything on the phone, and now I was here, practically with tail between my legs. But the reality was, I did really miss it here. Home and family. And perhaps it was Damon, despite our differences, who pushed me to realize that.

"I don't know, maybe I'll come back for good."

Megan's eyebrow arched in surprise. "Why would you do that?"

"I miss it a lot. I miss you guys. The boys are growing up. I feel like I've missed out on so much time already," I admitted.

She seemed to choose her next words carefully. "I appreciate and understand that. But you're not responsible for us, Clover."

I fell silent. *I'd done a bad job of that already.*

"Clover, I've always been so proud of your ability

to go for what you want. You moved us here to Ithaca, and then on to New York, following your dream. That's inspiring and magical. You're not made for a small place like this. Yes, you might be tired and *definitely* need a break. But you're not meant to be here. You need to look after yourself more. You don't have to worry about us, we're fine."

"But you know I promised Dad and you guys that I'd help this household when he passed away. I—"

"Mom and I are both fully grown women, Clover. The only person you should be looking after is yourself. You don't have to keep sending us money. Honestly, we're fine. The house is mostly paid off and I've got work now. You don't have to keep feeling obliged or guilty because you left. We're happy here. You never had to stay in that hell job for so long. Sure it's good money but look at what it's doing to you."

"I just..." My words fell flat. *I just what?* "I just feel so stuck right now. And—" I didn't want to end that sentence. I didn't want to think about Damon any more than I already had—already was. Every time his face came to mind, I was overwhelmed by mixed emotions and too embarrassed to admit how much I'd already fallen for him. I don't think I'd ever truly loved anyone before. But if it felt like this, then I wasn't sure I wanted any part of it.

"We need to talk about him, Clover. I've never seen you strung up about a guy like this before."

Me taking interest in someone was not something Megan would let go. No matter how desperately I might try to avoid the discussion. "What's there to say? I told you about him."

"Yea you told me he was an escort. You had lots of fun. You didn't know who he really was and then you found out and he's some hot billionaire. What you didn't express is how he made you *feel.* Or why it hurt so much forcing you to come all the way back home. Don't get me wrong, I'm happy to see you but you're a smart woman. If you really wanted to discover his identity sooner you could've or you would've stopped the escalation and seeing him."

"'Seeing him' seems very loosely used at this point," I scoffed.

"It doesn't matter how long you're with someone Clover, sometimes things just click. Enough for you to go on a weekend getaway with him to the Bahamas."

I looked away, she was right, but I was ignorant to admitting it. I wanted to hate him. This feeling... this amount of hurt... I'd never felt anything like it before and it grated on me how much it got under my skin. I wasn't in control of my thoughts because it was all consumed by *him*, making me feel like a crazy person.

"Love comes in many shapes and forms, Clover," Megan said, sounding more like our mother now than herself. "Maybe you feel unsettled because you don't know what a relationship looks like to *you*. Maybe you've been on your own for so long, that the moment you had an out, you took it and now you're thinking about running away."

I gaped at her. When did my younger sister seem so wise? Her last relationship had been far from ideal. Traumatizing even. I hated being on the sidelines, knowing what he used to do to her, the alcohol he'd consume and how his rage had frightened her. I was powerless to help her and the boys. And now I felt like I was powerless to help myself. To help how I felt or from the truth of her words resonating.

"With one of 'Manhattan's most desired billionaire bachelors.'" I air quoted. "I can't be involved in that kind of lifestyle. We came from nothing, Megan. Maybe I didn't care so much as to who he was because I always felt like it had an expiry date on it anyway. But the moment I realized *who* he was, it changed everything. I didn't feel like we were ever on equal terms at all. I felt like I was just some trivial plaything to him."

"Clover, look at me." I did—partially. Then I collected the cookie again, finding somewhere else to focus my attention. It hurt, again. Just thinking about it, saying it out loud. Admitting to the feelings that I pretended to push to the side. "Maybe much like you, he had his own reasons to enjoy the time spent. Now don't get me wrong, if he's a rich and pompous ass then I'll kick him to the curb for you. But I certainly won't allow you to try and push away the first guy you've found interest in for, well forever long, because you feel unworthy."

My gaze snapped on hers. *Unworthy?* No, I was hurt.

"I love you so much. You're one of the most smartest and beautiful woman I know. But you've let that confidence dwindle down to nothing after working for that boss of yours. It doesn't matter who or what background either of you come from. You're both human and you either have chemistry or you don't. Did he ever ask anything of you?"

I furrowed my eyebrows. "No."

"Then obviously who you are was more than enough. Sometimes, Clover, you don't have to bring things to the party—just yourself. And perhaps a part of you already knew that, that's why you didn't ask any more questions. You're an ex-journalist for goodness sake, if you wanted to know, you would've known, stop making excuses."

I was gobsmacked. It wasn't at all the sympathy I was expecting from my sister. "I'm surprised you're not wanting to join me on a pitchfork hunt for him," I admitted. Not because I wanted Damon to hurt, but because she seemed so calm, almost reflective in bringing things to my attention that perhaps I'd been too ignorant to admit.

"Because I'm grateful to him for at least sparking something in you again. It's the most alive I've seen you in years and it's nice to see you bubbling over with this emotion instead of braving that face you show everyone. Especially me and Mom. Yes, he might've been your undoing and possibly got you in trouble with work, which you know I don't like anyways. But the best lessons come from vulnerability. If you want to truly come back to Ithaca, you know Mom and I will welcome you with open arms. *But* I won't let you run back because you're scared to truly *feel* something. Now hurry up and eat that cookie before Mom gets back," she added, grabbing her own.

Cautiously, I took another bite, unsure if she'd

spiked it with something. My head was spinning. For the first time, I felt like Megan was acting like the older sister. I straightened my shoulders, trying to embody that confidence on again, realizing just like she said that after all these years it'd been a fake armor. And that left me feeling... uneasy. Had I been hiding all this time? Just going through the motions doing what I thought was "right"?

Chapter 32

Damon

I'd already knocked on Clover's door on two separate occasions with no response. Both times left me feeling more desperate and dejected. Was I coming across as some kind of stalker? She hadn't answered any of my calls, and so I gave up after the third ring. I just needed... to explain. *I just needed to hear her voice and make sure she was okay.*

I found myself wondering the streets with the urge to take in the fresh air and try to clear my mind. It just swivelled around one thing. Or more specifically one person.

My shoulders collided with a passerby as they hurriedly ran past. I looked over my shoulder, but the man was already gone. The shake of blonde curls grabbed my attention through a shabby restaurant window. Cassidy nodded with a plastered smile opposite a date. She stifled a yawn, trying her hardest to still seem interested in the conversation.

My legs were working of their own accord, barging into the restaurant. She looked up, her eyes going wide as I approached the table.

"Cassidy, can we talk for a minute?" I asked, near out of breath.

"Who's this guy?" the twenty-something-year-old demanded. Gel kept down his springy curls and his beard needed a trim ASAP. I squinted at the lip piercing before reaching his eyes, along with the effective glance I offered most people when they should find themselves busy elsewhere.

Cassidy sighed. "Sorry he's my ex-boyfriend, probably coming to apologize for being such a shitty boyfriend," she lied, though her clipped tone laced was laced with some truth. "Can you give us a minute?"

"Nah, man, I play for keeps. I'm not going anywhere."

Cassidy let out another long-winded sigh, lazily resting her chin on her hand. She looked at me then as if her current date wasn't even there. "You owe me a drink and are picking up the tab."

I nodded.

She gave the guy a smile. "Sorry, Tim, it's not going to work out. I think we're after different things in life. And if I'm being completely honest your profile looks very different."

"You shallow bitch," he snorted.

She seemed taken aback but held her own. "I'm not shallow. I just don't give a flying care about fish or the list of your ex-girlfriends who all did you dirty."

"You need to leave," I growled, impatient and holding in my bubbling anger at the way he spoke to her.

"Good, I was done here anyway," he grumbled, grabbing his denim jacket and barging past me. I let the shoulder hit go and briefly assessed where he sat for hygienic purposes before taking my own seat.

"Oh come on, he wasn't that bad, princess," Cassidy drawled out, her usually bouncy chipper self gone.

I cocked an uneven smile. "I've never seen this side of you."

"This is the side people see when they seriously piss me off and have hurt one of my friends," she chastised before calling over a waitress. "I'll have two of your most expensive cocktails." She glanced over me. "And what were you ordering?"

I quirked a smile. "Nothing for me." I waited for the waitress to leave before I added. "You can do better than that guy," I said casually.

"Ironic, coming from Mr. Liar."

"I didn't mean to lie," I gritted out. "And I'm not the only one keeping my family name a secret, am I now, Little Heiress?"

She was taken aback, an immediate show of shock and horror.

I quickly clarified, "I'm not going to tell anyone, that's your business."

She frowned looking at the near empty glass containing half-melted ice cubes. "It makes me feel no better than what you've done to her, when you put it like that."

"We all have our family secrets. And I'm not going to ask about yours."

The waitress strolled over with one blue and one red cocktail and placed them on the table. Cassidy smiled politely and watched the waitress walk away. "Why are you here, Damon?"

I let out an exasperated sigh, uncomfortable by my fisted hand under the table. I didn't want to come across as a desperate or mad man. And it'd been long since I was out of control- of myself or those around me. But my reality was, I was at my wit's end. I was *desperate* to see her—at least one last time. "I've tried her apartment twice and she's not there. I just need to talk to her."

"Well of course she's not there, Dummy. I'm house-sitting. She's gone back to Ithaca."

"What?"

"Yea her and Debra had a big blow up and after the article of you two went around she wanted to get away and go back home."

"For a visit?" My hand fisted harder.

Cassidy shrugged nonchalantly and took a sip from her straw. "By the sounds of it, she was considering moving back. I think for now a visit. But she might change her mind."

My stomach dropped, an unsettled feeling growing dire. "Do you know when she'll be back?"

"So far it's only meant to be a week. But things change."

Silence devoured the space. I couldn't go to Ithaca, could I? Wouldn't that make me a real stalker? But waiting out another week felt like eternity. I couldn't sleep as it was.

"It's not nice when somethings out of your control is it?" Cassidy asked. "I mean really, what did you think would happen? It boggles my mind that none of us figured it out sooner, but your identity was always going to be revealed. What did you think was going to happen?"

I sagged in my chair defeated. Both Michelle and Alex had said the same thing after I'd explained the full story to them. "I didn't think. I kept finding ways and excuses to see her. I just wanted to be with her. I didn't know who she was or worked for when I took that call. But afterwards I couldn't help myself. Everything else about my life was complicated I didn't want to throw her into it as well. Everything my family did was scrutinized. It didn't seem fair."

"But you also can't make that decision for her," Cassidy said before taking a satisfied slurp of her cocktail. Cassidy's eyes danced. "You're in love with her, aren't you?"

"Yes." The response was out before I even had time to think about it. I felt the thickness lodge in my throat as if it might suffocate me. I'd been so blind. Of course I did. Or why else would I be at my wit's end trying to rectify this? I'd never flipped half the city overlooking for someone. The realization dawned on me as to how wrong I'd been about everything.

"You have a funny way of showing it," Cassidy

said, now finished with the first drink. "But now you have some time to put your words together before she comes back. But you only get one shot, if she says no, I don't want to see you around her again." She stood up with an edgy glare.

Confused and with a coy smile, I asked. "Are you threatening me there, little Cassidy?"

She harrumphed, throwing her small handbag over her shoulder. "Threatening's a bit steep. But I am protective of her. She deserves someone who makes her happy. And if she decides that's not you then you need to step aside. Here, have a drink. I'll be rooting for you." She scooted the untouched drink my way and sauntered out.

And now, I sat alone at a restaurant after ruining someone else's date, desperate to find Clover's whereabouts. Now that I knew, I felt more anxious. *What if she didn't come back?* What if she never forgives me? What if Cassidy was right and there was a better man waiting for Clover? Perhaps it was only right that I stepped aside.

Chapter 33

Clover

"Forgive me, but I must confess, I find it strange why you wanted to meet with me," I admitted to Michelle. I'd only just arrived back in Manhattan after six days with my family. It didn't feel like it was enough time, and yet I had to face the chaos and clean up what I'd left behind.

She'd chosen a reasonably central café and arrived first. When I walked in, she was busily discussing a serious matter on the phone. I didn't know what to make of the brilliant woman sitting before me as we ordered our coffees.

She was someone I imagined people were sucked into following quickly. Much like her brother, she had a certain presence about her. When listening to her on the phone, I recognized her brisk efficiency. We had the same work ethic, but she seemed more confident in her pointed direction. I mean, after all, she was the CEO of *Be True*. Perhaps she was also a woman who wasn't accustomed to dropping anything without notice. I imagined she too was used to being in control.

"Much like my brother, I'm also direct and we both get that from our father," she started. At my obvious uncomfortableness at the mention of her brother, she quickly added, "But I'm not here to discuss my brother with you. That's yours and his business. What I am interested in is your work." She leant forward.

"Sorry?"

"I was intrigued. After I spoke with you and my brother separately. I know a good writer when I see one. I looked through your old portfolio. I'm not igno-rant to the gossip I hear of Debra Coorman. Sure, she maintains a nice empire, but she has a delicate ego and it's my understanding that you've been unfairly treated because of that."

I took a sip of my coffee. *Where was she going with this?*

"In short, despite the conflict of interest you might have with my brother, I'm also a person who sees potential and opportunity within others and how it might best serve my own company. I'd like to offer you a job, Clover, as a travel columnist."

My jaw dropped. *Was this some kind of pity for her brother's sake?*

"With all respect, I really appreciate the offer. But there's a lot involved with this, especially because of your brother. Did he ask you to do this for me?" I immediately felt conceited for even asking. He probably hadn't thought of me twice since the Bahamas. So why was she trying to drag me back in?

"No. And at my suggestion, if it's easier initially you can freelance, if you'd like to avoid him. Though it may be hard considering he is co-owner. But the role is there if you'd like it. I read your work and was impressed by it on its own. This is from woman to woman. A company extending an opportunity to a talented writer." She took a sip of her black coffee, her expression not giving anything away.

I looked past her long lashes and into her dark eyes, eyes that reminded me of Damon. I'd agreed to this meeting not at all knowing what to expect. But this certainly was the last thing.

"You already have so many fantastic writers," I quickly found myself saying. "Why me?"

"Well only when they write," she rolled her eyes.

"But you have a unique humor in your writing that I quite like. I think it would work well in our magazine and audience. We're working on a few things to freshen our current team and projects."

I considered this, flattered. I was curious about one thing, perhaps it was intertwined. "I heard that Anonymous hadn't written in last week's online magazine. Is that why you're looking for more writers?"

She studied me carefully, a coy smile lighting her face. "How interesting that you read our magazine and are familiar with that writer." She took another sip. "You do realize that Damon writes those pieces."

My jaw dropped.

"And ever since the Bahamas he's been rather useless at anything at all." She placed her coffee cup back down. "I know it's not my place to say, but I do think my brother cares for you deeply. Despite how you might've met, I think his intent was genuine. I haven't seen him like this with anyone for quite some time now."

"He told you how we really met?" I asked quietly, suddenly fascinated with the sugar and swirling it into my coffee, even though I usually don't add it into my already sweet lattes.

"The escorting? Admittedly, I thought he'd

stopped that a long time ago," she said with a heavy sigh.

I didn't want to talk about Damon, nor did I want that to monopolize the opportunity just offered, and yet I couldn't help myself asking quietly, "How did he become an escort?"

The reality was, I didn't want to ask him that question and might never have the opportunity to.

"He hasn't told you yet, huh?" she asked, surprised. I gave her a pointed look to indicate that he hadn't. Amongst many other things. She was reluctant to say anything, and I thought she wouldn't. But after another long sip, she said, "I can't say exactly why my brother might've remained quiet about his identity but what I do know is he had no intention of hurting you. And the escorting stuff. That was my idea, actually. When he'd found himself in a public scandal and issues with his ex and best friend at the time, he was a mess. He thought he'd dishonored the family and company, but he didn't really care for himself. He just kind of faded into the shadows.

"I started to worry about him and he refused to go out and meet anyone new. One of my friends had no one to take her to a masquerade event, so I suggested he take her. He was turning into a real miserable bastard. I thought it would do him good to get out of the office, and, well, I thought he might meet someone eventually. My friend insisted that she pay him, and after that, it slowly started becoming a regular thing. I didn't much understand it either. We even got into a fight about it once. But he swore he was only escorting them and nothing more. But mostly, he was doing it for his writing."

"Writing?" That piqued my interest as I tried to make sense of the rest of his story. What a complicated way to find inspiration for his stories, and yet they'd always been so sensitive and cleverly written. Had he found the opportunity to mask himself and simply observe far more compelling than his everyday life?

"When our mother was diagnosed with cancer, my father wanted to be by her side, so he offered the CEO position to Damon. This was all happening about the time he and Annabelle split, so he offered it to me. But I wanted it to be our legacy and family business. Despite how much we squabbled, growing up we also used to do everything together. Although I might be the face of the company now, Damon is always silently working in the background. Everyone who works for us knows his input weighs as equally as mine. But he always loved writing as well. So, he decided to trial his articles in a few editions and readers loved the mysterious identity. He's written ever since, well until now."

Michelle's cell began to vibrate but she ignored it. "I do appreciate you coming to meet me, Clover. I know it would've been a difficult thing. And even though I said we wouldn't talk about my brother, here we are." She rolled her eyes, as if he monopolized everything. It brought a genuine smile to my face. I wondered how many people saw this side of the renowned *Be True* CEO.

"I appreciate everything you've said," I offered sincerely. The truth was, a small part of me, under the embarrassment and uncertainty, was relieved to think that maybe Damon wasn't doing too well just like me. And that made me feel all mixed feelings— hope and silly all at the same time.

"I'd like to be upfront about something. I'm currently considering moving back to Ithaca and what you've offered me is an opportunity of a lifetime. Can you give me a few days to think about it?"

"Of course," Michelle said, almost disappointed. "Take as long as you need. I am sorry again though for what happened."

I placed my empty mug on the table and offered her a smile. Last time I'd seen her I was running barefoot to get as far away from her brother and family name as quickly as possible. And now they'd offered me my dream job. The irony wasn't lost.

But I needed time to think—about all of it—because my mind had found no conclusion in Ithaca. And tomorrow I was due back at my day job, confined by everything that'd slowly chipped away at me in the last two years. "I appreciate you saying that Michelle and I'll let you know either way what I've decided. Thank you."

Chapter 34

Clover

S tepping into the tall, I pulled back my shoulders confidently and made my way across the white marble floors to the recep-tionist inquiring what level the *Candice* event was being hosted on. She quickly explained to me that it was on the third floor and a few guests had already arrived.

Waiting patiently in the elevator, I wondered why we had to invite partners along to these events. Debra wanted to make it as informal as possible so that our sponsors felt like they were part of a family. In my opinion, it was a waste of money. But maybe I thought that because I was in a bitter mood. It had never bothered me before. It was after all my first day back in the office and I really didn't want to put the old poker face on anymore. It all just felt so tiring now.

When the elevator opened, two large wooden doors were revealed across the hall. There were a few guests in the room beyond, standing around and sipping on their drinks. Very few looked up from their idle chatter as I entered the room.

I noticed Debra and her husband, Gary, and stepped in the other direction. I grabbed a glass of champagne and knocked half the contents back, less elegantly than I'd like to admit. We hadn't spoken since our last blowout and part of me anticipated her to publicly humiliate me in some way. Or make a snide remark or be up to her old tricks. And I just didn't have the will power in me anymore to just roll over and take it. My sister had been right about one thing, her and my mom were okay without my financial help. I'd since learnt they'd just been saving the money into an account for the last year. Ultimately, I'd only jeopardized my own health, using them as an excuse for necessity when all along I should've stood up for myself sooner. *Candice* was a great opportunity once, but now I'd become bitter toward it.

One of the sponsor's wives I'd previously met

approached me first. Nula was a lovely woman and a fitness fanatic. She had tight blonde curls and a body to die for. She looked stunning for a fifty-year-old woman. Like last time, she commented on my shape and how I might "sculpt" it through minimal eating and exercising. I nodded in politeness as I gulped another mouthful of my drink.

We were interrupted by Gary who came to join in the conversation. He seemed more than happy to look me over as Nula explained how to do squats properly. When she left to fetch her husband, Gary and I were once again left alone in awkward conversation.

"You look stunning tonight," he said shyly. "You look like you've lost weight."

"Clean eating," I said sarcastically, instantly regretting my unfair tone. It wasn't Gary's fault I was in the grumps. I was just so over playing this part.

"Ah, Clover, glad you could make it," Debra said, quickly clinging to her husband's arm. "But no Damon, I see?" And I was sick of playing this particular game with this woman who drove me crazy.

"Like I said last time, Damon and I are finished," I said, swirling my champagne in agitation. But she already knew that.

Her thin lips curled into a smile before she composed herself again. "Oh, how sad. He was rather charming. Although I did wonder how long it could last for," she said facetiously to Gary, making the atmosphere awkward. I smiled, holding back my fierce words as I swallowed the last of my champagne.

"Don't be jealous of her just because your husband so obviously wants her," Damon's voice echoed from behind. Electricity ran up my spine, stiffening me into position. If I turned around, he might be standing there. Or he might not be. My heart pounded. Could I face him now? Or was I just hopeful I'd heard his voice?

Slowly and disbelieving I turned around. He was wearing long black pants, pointed polished shoes, and a long-sleeved, button-up white shirt. My breath hitched, as it always did when I saw him. Except I'd never thought I'd see him again.

"Gary does not *want* her!" Debra said, her voice breaking. I stared at her, noticing her broken composure. I couldn't help but glance at Gary now, who was shuffling uncomfortably where he stood.

Is that why Debra treated me the way she did... because she thought I was a threat? I thought of all the things she had done to make my working life hell,

all because she was *jealous*. Was that why she made
such an obvious play for Damon?

Gary looked at me and then away from the group
as red blushed across his cheeks. He fumbled for
words, but found none. I recalled Damon suggesting
this to me once before. But it was Gary and Debra's
broken composure that confirmed it. How had I over-
looked it? *Because I was never looking for it,* I
thought.

I thought we were all just playing a part at these
events and social gatherings. I turned from them,
locking onto the bigger question I had right then as
my heart unnaturally pounded in my chest. "What
are you doing here, Damon?" I asked, his name
causing a lump in my throat.

"I was hoping we might be able to have a word
outside," Damon said uncomfortably as onlookers
ogled us.

Debra was seething. "The Brogardts are not
invited to this event. If you don't leave of your own
accord, I'll call security."

"I'm not leaving without Clover," he said in his
rough, unmoving tone. I shuffled uncomfortably,
wanting to protect myself from the vulnerability that
was about to display itself. I couldn't handle the risk
of being humiliated and rejected again, especially in

front of all these people. And I didn't want a big ordeal being made again like that stupid article from the Bahamas.

I looked around the room. Everyone was gaping at us interested. He wasn't using his usual dark shades, because he wasn't hiding his identity anymore, I realized. Even if I asked Damon to leave, he'd say his part in front of them all, with little embarrassment. I nodded and made my way for the door.

We walked silently down the hall to another conference room, away from eavesdropping distance at least. Damon walked behind me, his hands in his pockets. When he closed the door behind us in the dully lit room, I turned on him. "You have no right to be here," I said angrily, though my heart rapidly pounded to finally see him again. My body betrayed my logical sense in every way. He'd humiliated me, and yet just by seeing him now, I still wanted him. I was angrier at myself than him.

"I know. After my sister told me you were thinking of moving to Ithaca, I found myself here. I was going to wait until you were home tonight but I needed to see you and apologize. I've been needing to apologize to you ever since that day. I'm sorry, Clover. It wasn't meant to be like that."

"But it was," I said, scorned as my body tried to betray me. I wanted to touch him, to slap him, to kick, to scream, to cry—all of those emotions mixing into a tangible lump in my throat.

"I never explained who I was because we started through the escort business. And then past that, I didn't want to drag you into the responsibility of what being associated with my family was like. I didn't realize what I'd felt until it was too late." He licked his lips, his eyes taking in every small motion of my body. I crossed my arms, preparing to put my guard further up. I hinged on every word he said with a mixture of anger, anguish, and hope. "I tried to forget everything that happened. But I couldn't, and it's been eating at me ever since. You deserved at least an explanation and apology. And then I felt guilty for wanting you after what I did. I wasn't deserving enough of you. It's been torture these last few weeks. I haven't been able to get you out of my mind, and well"—he threw his hands in the air flabbergasted—"that's how I wound up here. I just wanted... I just wanted to see you."

He looked at me, desperately searching for a response. I tried to hold a poker face. "You humiliated me. I could've lost my job. And I felt so stupid."

"I know," he said miserably. "I hate what I did to

you. I swear, Clover, I've never been this frantic to make something right." He cautiously stepped toward me. The large space between us closed in further. "The time I spent with you, it was sincere. I haven't felt like that with any other woman, and I was too slow to realize myself what was happening. I thought that someone like you didn't exist. Especially not for me. I've never met anyone like you, and I panicked."

"How do I know it wasn't just research for Anonymous?" I asked bitterly. It had been in the back of my mind since I'd spoken to Michelle. What if I was just another woman to inspire his writing? Although I'd used him for a very specific purpose, I was embarrassed at the thought of being used in return. I worried that everything I felt was one-sided and I'd believed in a dreamlike scenario because, well I really liked him. As much as I hated the lump in my throat, a small part of me hung onto the bitter taste of hope.

He looked taken aback by my comment, surprised that I knew about his writing and why he became an escort in the first place. "No, it was never like that with you. When I started escorting I did it because it enabled me to experience events and being by a woman's side, not distracted by romance.

I've never led anyone on. There was a clear boundary of payment of services to differentiate from that. And yes, it did inspire a lot of my writing."

Tears welled in my eyes, a bitter and awful type of jealousy springing to mind. He'd escorted so many women before, why was I hopeful I'd be different? That old voice and reminder of feeling little and insignificant rose once again.

"You were never that," he said powerfully, grabbing my attention and cutting any fleeting thoughts I might've had. "I wanted to be around you, but you terrified me. Around you I couldn't keep my composure, everything in my life was set, and yet when I had the chance to see you, I took it. For the first time in my life, I couldn't control myself. That terrified me, Clover," he said, his voice raw. "I have thought of that day over and over in my head, regretting it. I never thought after doing that to you that I deserved to fight for you. You were never a project for me. I just wanted to be with you, and I was too stupid to realize it."

A tear slid down my face as I tried to control my quivering bottom lip. He took another step forward, his voice breaking. "Clover, please. You have to believe me."

I didn't have to believe anything, even when he

begged so vulnerably. *But I did.* Because I now understood that sense of vulnerability and scarcity. But what if he was tricking me now? What if my heart was ruling my decision? I found no greater answer because deep down since the moment I ran away, I'd hoped he'd chase me, embarrassingly so. Desperate and hopeful, I felt akin to him and so badly wished it had worked. I wanted to stand behind my logic, but my heart screamed at me to embrace him, to calm his nerves and tell him it would be all right.

I couldn't choke out a word, scared that I would betray my strong stance that was now crumbling. How did he hold such power over me?

He took the last step between us and my breath hitched. "I'm so sorry, Clover," he said, his voice quivering. He raised his hand slowly to my cheek, cupping my face and wiping away one of the tears that fell. I felt timid, wanting to flinch away from him but unable to do so. I closed my eyes, my body betraying me as I savored the callouses on his hands. I felt like I had taken my first full breath in the last few weeks.

"I will never forgive myself for doing that to you. But I realized—even without my sister telling me—

how much of a mistake I had made and how much of an idiot I'd been.

"I want to be near you, laughing with you, having you in the same room as me. I haven't wanted anything else as desperately. You bring a calm to my life, Clover, that no one else could replicate."

He cupped his other hand around my other cheek, his dark-brown, molten eyes earnest. "I've only known you for such a short time, but already I know I want you in my life. I feared falling for you and not being wanted in return. I was scared and ran like a coward," he said. "And then I realized it was already too late because I'd already fallen for you. I only want you and the chance to get to know you properly. And I came here preparing myself for whatever answer you might give me."

I looked at him longingly, my legs feeling as if they were going to collapse at any moment. Every word he spoke was raw and vulnerable. We all had our insecurities, and I was contending with my own now.

"Please, Clover, say something," he whispered, holding me fiercely. But it wasn't logic that wanted to speak. My body spoke its truth, my heart pattering with every second surrounded by his scent, presence and passion. From the day I had met him, my life had changed. *I had changed.*

I curled my hand around the back of his neck and pulled him in for a kiss. His lips parted, gently and lovingly, not with the fever we found ourselves in previously between sheets, but rather a delicate exploration. Something my body had ached for, for so long. It felt right kissing Damon, perfectly matched and my body only hungrily craved more.

"You took so long," I said as I pulled back breathlessly, tears tumbling down my face. Damon swept them away, a sigh of relief escaping him.

"I know," he agreed as we both smiled sheepishly. "I should've never hidden it away from you. But when you ran, you took every part of me with you. You win, Clover, I'm crazy for you."

His words lingered in the air, my heart aching with them. I rubbed my hand against his unshaven jaw and smiled foolishly at his confession. *I've won.* Because at the start it was just a game, but quite quickly we threw both our hearts on the line without realizing until it was too late.

Damon's face brightened and his eyes danced as the traces of a cocky smile pulled at his mouth. He swept me off my feet, a small squeal passing through my lips as I felt the weight of the world effortlessly drip off my shoulders. He kissed me again, looking at me longingly. "Now, we have some unfinished business to attend to," he growled.

I smiled at him wickedly, the fire spreading through my body once again, a flame that would only burn for him. *My Escort.*

Epilogue – Clover

I hadn't even heard or felt the buzz of my phone as I missed Damon's calls. The last text read, *I hope you're having a good night, my beautiful Buttercup. Sorry I missed the chance to hear your sexy voice. We'll talk tomorrow. I love you. And don't miss your sexy god of a boyfriend, or charming orange cat. We're still eating only the best salmon.* There was a little emoticon of a mischievous grin. I couldn't help but laugh at the stupidity of it.

With Damon staying in Manhattan, he opted to look after Pudding instead of Cassidy, though she didn't mind house-sitting my apartment. Damon hardly text, let alone sent emoticons. And it came as no surprise to me that he'd recently found the mischievous grin emoji. I tried calling him, before quickly hanging up when I realized what the time was. It was already 1:08 a.m. in his time zone. *Shit. I hope I didn't wake him.* I replied back, *I love you, and I could never forget about my sexy, obnoxious cat and my boyfriend.* A satisfied smile curled my lips. I'd be flying out from Hawaii tomorrow with most of this piece already written.

It was nice to be traveling so often, refreshing even. I pulled the blankets over me as the chill of night rolled over. But the truth was, it felt almost empty without having Damon here. I splayed out my hand in the part of the bed he would've slept in. By now he would've pulled me in from behind and wrapped me in his warmth. It'd only been two months since everything had changed. I took the job at *Be True* magazine and I'd never looked back. There was no other way to look other than in Damon's direction.

We'd begun to navigate our new life together, including the whims of photographers and random articles coming out. But since working with the boss from hell at *Candice,* I realized I'd learnt how to build armor around myself, deflecting their gossip and choosing to focus on my truth and what was important instead. And as quickly as I'd fallen for Damon, we gravitated around one another and our busy careers like it'd suck us in whole. We could never escape one another, even if we tried. And for that, I was grateful.

I was also grateful for my decision to stay in Manhattan with Damon and honor what we had between us. To really live again and to understand what it meant to love and be loved. And no matter how strange our meeting, or the broken miscommunication between, our feelings for one another spoke louder than any newspaper article or social media gossip.

Damon had hung his hat up in his escorting days, satisfied with his last client and now girlfriend and focused on growing the Brogardt business. I shuffled the pillow and laid my head down, excited to see Damon tomorrow and remind him of all the wicked things we'd share over the coming days and nights.

Damon

"You left me for four days," I growled into Clover's ear. There was something sexy about her being in my office, her ass propped against my wooden desk. I nuzzled into her neck, nibbling at one of her sensitive spots.

"Damon," she whispered, almost begging. "It's your company that sent me there."

"True, but I wanted you here all to myself." My hand crept up her outer leg, the pencil skirt doing nothing to deter my imagination. "And Pudding scratched me twice."

The rich vibration of her laughter ran over me like a charming snake. It always rendered me useless, unable to say no to her and unable to deny the immediate demand of my body wanting her closer to mine.

"It's good to see you two are getting along better," she toyed.

"Cheeky, my little Angel Puff," I taunted.

Squabbling erupted outside my office door. Alex and Sotiny's constant arguing becoming background noise as they approached my office. I couldn't help but find amusement in it. Michelle said they were always on their best behavior in the main office and around her. Admittedly, I enjoyed watching a woman bust Alex's nerves—his usual calm, charismatic self coming undone.

I pressed one more gentle kiss to Clover's throat as they busted into the room and immediately paused. Clover casually pushed me back, that underlying humor glimmering in her gaze.

"We should come back," Sotiny said, grabbing Alex's hand and spinning back toward the door.

He seemed just as surprised by the gesture. "We're fine," I laughed. Clover shuffled off the desk and pressed a kiss to my cheek, straightening the collar of my shirt.

"That's all I had to report," she said with a smile. "See you tonight?"

My smile spread. "I have nowhere else I'd rather be." She sauntered out of the room, her confidence over the last few weeks blossoming as she became more comfortable in her new office.

As if his hand was burning her, Sotiny flicked Alex away. "We just wanted to report that Hayden Zilch will be coming in for a meeting, we'll be scheduling a time and day that best suits him but he has alluded to the coming month."

Clover paused at the door. "Hayden Zilch?" she asked over her shoulder.

"Yea, he's a bigwig sports manager. From your hometown actually in Ithaca," Alex added. He really liked Clover and respectfully kept his jokes minimal around her. I wasn't a jealous man, but I also treasured what was mine and *only* mine.

"I know who he is. He was my best friend in university. You're bringing him on board?" she asked me with excitement dancing in her gaze. My heart squeezed with an unfamiliar tension.

"Possibly. We're expanding."

"Wow. What a small world, I look forward to seeing him. It's been years." She wandered off into her own thoughts. "Oh, sorry I'll leave you. Have a good day."

"I wonder if she realizes her university buddy is still a sex god on legs," Alex commented, waiting for my reaction with a mischievous grin. He was purposefully poking me.

Sotiny tsked. "It might shock you that women value something more than a muscled body and pretty face. Like... I don't know... a nice personality."

"That would involve getting to know someone well enough to see if they had one, wouldn't it?" he shot back.

"Sometimes there isn't any more to see other than what they've already got on offer. Not everyone has depth," she harrumphed. Tension laced the room.

My cell buzzed in my pocket and when I looked down at a subtle text from Clover, I hid my smirk. *My meeting doesn't start for another twenty minutes. Come find me.*

A low guttural growl escaped me, trying to prevent my arousal. We'd found a safe little spot that wasn't interrupted by anyone. It might've been a small closet, but it was all we needed. I felt like a teenager again, unable to keep my hands to myself and chasing her around like she was the very air I breathed.

I interrupted the two who'd become lost in their own sparring. "I look forward to it and you've compiled the notes and details for the meeting?"

As if suddenly realizing I was still in the room with them, Sotiny straightened. "Yes and we've emailed it to you as well. We wanted to tell you in person before the meeting."

"Perfect. I appreciate your efforts. Looks like times are changing around here. Now if you'll excuse me, I need to grab a coffee before my next meeting."

Sotiny nodded, not looking Alex's way a second time. He hovered by the door. "Is this the same excuse as last time, when you didn't come to the meeting with a coffee in hand?"

I couldn't contain my small male smirk.

"It's good to see you like this again, you think she's the one huh?" he asked.

"Without a doubt." And the truth was I'd never been surer of anything else in my life. I could feel it in my entire being. Clover was mine to have. "Maybe you should try it sometime, you're not getting any younger," I jabbed with a smile.

Alex shook his head as I made my escape down the hallway. And the truth was, ever since they started this project together, Sotiny was all he vented about during our sparring at the boxing gym. And I imagined that he lay awake at night tormented by the woman as well. The two had serious tension and history.

But that was for them to figure out. I had my own woman to please.

About the Author

Raised in the Darling Downs Region in Queensland, Australia, Kia Carrington-Russell, began writing as an angsty teenager, finding a passion for exploring creative realities and world building at fifteen. After graduating high school she decided to pursue a career in freelance journalism, and quickly amended that dream with something that made her heart beat faster and her mind race—fiction. With fresh eyes she went over her first manuscript, "Possession of my Soul" and began her publishing journey in 2014.

With a recognizable style of kick ass heroines, fast-paced action, and romance that dances from light to dark, she's been pronounced "the new up and coming author to look out for" and her writing style as "hauntingly beautiful."

Carrington-Russell's books have been recognized on multiple best-seller lists, most noticeably, her "Token Huntress" and "My Escort" series for which she's won numerous awards and notable reviews, including "Reader's Favorite" 5 star reviews for

"Token Huntress" and "The Shadow Minds Journal."

She has a firm belief in giving back to the writing community—sharing knowledge, promotions, and opportunities that might help other authors reach their readers, including running her own YouTube channel, Bound by Books, where she interviews fellow authors and other industry professionals.

With years in various industries, climbing the corporate ladders, Kia has now settled into a full-time writing career as a successful author and is always looking for the next adventure. She's travelled the world for both business and pleasure, including living in Edinburgh, Scotland for the past year.

Now back in her home country of Australia, she takes her Cavoodle, Sia along morning walks on beautiful coastline beaches, building worlds in the sea breezes and contemplating where she'll go next.

To connect find Kia on www.kiacarrington-russell.com